# The Grumpy Cowboy Next Door

A Sweet, Small Town Romance:
Book One in the Sugar Plum Series

## Ava Wakefield

Ava Wakefield Romance, LLC

**Copyright © 2024 by Ava Wakefield Romance, LLC**

All rights reserved.

No portion of this book may be reproduced, duplicated, or transmitted in electronic or printed format without written permission from the publisher except as permitted by U.S. copyright law.

Respective authors own all copyrights not held by the publisher.

# Contents

1. Chapter One — 1
2. Chapter Two — 9
3. Chapter Three — 18
4. Chapter Four — 26
5. Chapter Five — 33
6. Chapter Six — 41
7. Chapter Seven — 47
8. Chapter Eight — 55
9. Chapter Nine — 65
10. Chapter Ten — 71
11. Chapter Eleven — 79
12. Chapter Twelve — 87
13. Chapter Thirteen — 95
14. Chapter Fourteen — 102
15. Chapter Fifteen — 109
16. Chapter Sixteen — 115
17. Chapter Seventeen — 123

| | | |
|---|---|---|
| 18. | Chapter Eighteen | 131 |
| 19. | Chapter Nineteen | 137 |
| 20. | Chapter Twenty | 145 |
| 21. | Chapter Twenty-One | 154 |
| 22. | Chapter Twenty-Two | 161 |
| 23. | Chapter Twenty-Three | 168 |
| 24. | Chapter Twenty-Four | 175 |
| 25. | Chapter Twenty-Five | 181 |
| 26. | Chapter Twenty-Six | 188 |
| 27. | Chapter Twenty-Seven | 194 |
| 28. | Chapter Twenty-Eight | 200 |
| 29. | Chapter Twenty-Nine | 206 |
| 30. | Chapter Thirty | 213 |
| 31. | Epilogue | 220 |
| 32. | More Clean Romance from Ava | 227 |

# Chapter One

**Gemma**

"There's no easy way to say this. You have retrograde amnesia."

I blink hard at the stranger in the white lab coat.

"You may not remember some, or most, of your old memories. But the good news is that you can make new ones, and there's always a chance your old ones can return. Do you have any questions?"

If my situation wasn't so insane, I might crack a laugh at the last words my doctor says before I agree to hop on a plane with a man who claims to be my dad and let him take me "home."

Do I have any questions? Uh.... *Yeah!* When am I going to wake up from this nightmare?

After a short layover in Houston and a final touchdown in Lubbock, we weave through the airport parking lot to a faded red pickup truck that looks older than I am, and I can't help but wonder if it's going to make it for the remaining hour and a half drive to my alleged hometown.

"I know you're tired, but we'll be home before you know it." Henry Carter, a man who shares my last name as well as my green eyes, pulls my door open for me, and it gives a soft creak.

I stare at the passenger's seat for a moment, unable to move. I can only guess that going back home is my best bet for remembering the past, but I'd be lying if I said I wasn't skeptical. What in the world am I going to remember?

*And who am I?*

Once inside and buckled up, we hit the road, leaving any remnants of civilization behind us in exchange for miles of wind turbines and a seemingly endless horizon. The trip lasts for what feels like an eternity, and I wonder if we will ever make it there.

"We're almost home," he says.

"What's that smell?" I cover my nose and mouth with my hand to block out a pungent smell that can only be likened to—

"Feedlots. There's a lot of them around these parts, but don't worry. You'll get used to it."

As the truck rumbles down a stretch of abandoned highway, I peer out the hazy window and catch sight of an old wooden sign looming ahead that reads "Welcome to Sugar Plum."

"What's going to happen when we get home?" I ask, nervously twisting a short lock of wavy brown hair around my finger. When I notice the strands of gold, auburn, and platinum blonde that streak through, I pull down the passenger side visor and give a quick glance in the mirror at the textured layers framing my face. I may be having the worst week of my life, but at least my hair is on point.

The doctor recommended therapy, but I have no idea what that will look like. Judging by the size of Sugar Plum's town square, I'd be surprised if there were any rehab facilities nearby. It seems more like the kind of place where the only doctor in town moonlights as the town vet.

My father offers a comforting look, and I hold his gaze long enough to study his features. I imagine he's in his late forties with thick, wavy brown hair streaked with silver. He's built tall and thin but muscular, and his large hands look leathery and calloused as he lightly drums them over the steering wheel. Except for a thick mustache that grows from one dimple to the other and completely hides his upper lip, his face is clean-shaven, and his features are sharp.

"Well, Peanut—that's what your maw and I used to call you. You don't mind, do you?"

*Peanut?* The name sounds as unfamiliar as a cow reciting the alphabet. But I nod and decide to try it on for size. Anything to help me remember... right?

"I mentioned we own a family ranch," he continues. I nod again, remembering the painful conversation we had on the plane where he told me how my mother died before I moved away. "You'll be staying in the same house you grew up in. Your room is just like you left it, and I'm hoping after we get you all situated, maybe it'll help you remember things. Until then, I figure my ranch hand, Asher, can get you started with riding lessons first thing in the morning."

I lift an eyebrow at him and try to hide any hint of panic from my voice. "Riding lessons? As in... *horseback* riding?"

His eyes light up as he chuckles. "You always did love horses, and Doc said to immerse you in old passions. Thought riding again might help."

Did I really ride horses? Boy, this day keeps getting stranger by the minute. It's so weird knowing I used to love something I have no recollection of ever doing. Then again, I don't remember anything I used to do. All I know is that my name is Gemma Carter. I grew up in Sugar Plum, Texas, currently live in New York City, and got into a car accident where I hit my head and lost all my memories. How's *that* for my life in a nutshell?

After another five minutes of driving in silence, Henry turns off the main road and continues down a long dirt drive until two ranch-style houses, a large barn, a stable, and a field full of cows and other farm animals come into view.

I roll down the window to take in the fresh air. It's like a little slice of Heaven with its wispy grass, a small pond in the distance, and a very *tall*, very *large* man standing outside to greet us. I know Henry says everything is bigger in Texas, but with shoulders that broad, someone needs to write that man a ticket for concealed carry without a permit.

"This is it, Peanut—home sweet home. There's Asher now," Dad says, throwing the old Chevy into park. He gets out and comes around to open my door. "Asher, come meet my daughter."

As he approaches, I get a better look and remind myself to pick up my jaw off the floor. Though filthy, he's pretty handsome in his brown cowboy hat, jeans, and white t-shirt. I can tell he's been working hard by the sweat ring around his collar and the line of dirt across his forehead where his hat meets. Maybe horseback riding lessons won't be so bad… assuming he showers first.

"This is Gemma. You'll be teaching her how to ride."

"So… big city girl wants to get on a horse now, does she?" Asher raises an eyebrow and looks me up and down just before turning and spitting on the ground beside him.

*Eww, gross!*

Henry lets out a bellowing laugh and slaps Asher on the back. "Don't mind him, Gemma. Those cowboys from Nashville like pulling legs. Fortunately for me, this one's the best roper on this side of the Mississippi."

I ignore what I assume is my father's attempt at an apology on Asher's behalf and wrinkle my nose. I'm not sure I like Asher's judgmental tone or the fact that he just met me and is already making assumptions. "I'm standing right here," I say, shooting icy daggers as I look him dead in the eye.

Asher smirks then crosses his arms over his broad chest. "I know."

I feel my teeth begin to grind as I narrow my eyes. Do I really have to put up with this? And of all people, my father chose *him* to be my guide on my trip down memory recovery lane.

Great. This is going to be *so* much fun.

"You two play nice, now. I have to hop on a call, but Asher will show you to your room. I'm sorry I don't have time to show you around myself, but dinner is at six. We can catch up more after you've had a chance to get settled," Dad says. "I'm glad you're home, Gemma." He squeezes my shoulder and offers a tired smile—like he's the one glad to be back home finally.

The tension in my brow melts as I nod and return the smile. He's been nothing but kind to me, and for all I know, I may not even deserve it. He was my emergency contact at the hospital, so I know we must have some kind of relationship. But still, I wonder what made me leave and why he hasn't told me more about my life in New York.

When Dad is out of sight, I turn to Asher, who examines me like a foreign specimen. I know I must stick out like a sore thumb around here. Putting my silk blouse, designer shoes, and handbag next to his dusty boots and denim only proves the obvious difference in lifestyle choices. I just wish I could remember what that lifestyle was for me.

Asher escorts me toward the main house but seems cold and distant. Feeling the tension return to my forehead, I opt for small talk.

"How long have you worked on the ranch?"

I have to remove my heels and go barefoot to catch up to Asher, who doesn't bother slowing his pace as he climbs the porch steps, taking two at a time. The wood creaks slightly with every step, but despite the sounds of aging, the house is a beautiful single-story design with a wide profile.

The front porch is spacious and wraps around both sides of the house, with wood railings around the perimeter and rustic wooden columns offering support. The windows are large with shutters, and the front door looks heavy with a wrought iron handle and knocker. I even noticed a cute stone chimney nestled on the back of the metal roof when we pulled up to the house earlier.

"Few years. I'm probably one of the few folks in town who don't know you from before." Asher replies. I pause at the top of the steps and think about an entire town of strangers knowing who I am. It's a thought that makes my skin prickle. "Well, come on. I got things to do." Asher pushes the front door open and motions for me to follow behind.

He leads me inside, and I faintly hear my dad's voice coming from another room.

"I can't believe it either. I haven't seen her since she left at eighteen… I'm just glad she's home. I don't care about the past."

I frown, wondering if I'm in the wrong for eavesdropping, but I'm twenty-six now. Why haven't we seen each other for eight years?

"This way," Asher says. He hangs a left and stops at a closed-door just around the corner. "This is you."

"I'm surprised you know which one is mine," I say, amazed by how many doors they were able to squeeze into this place.

Asher meets my gaze with soft blue eyes that send a jolt of electricity shooting down my spine—a stark contrast against his hardened exterior. "Only door in the house Mr. Carter wants kept shut. Wasn't hard to put two and two together. But… if you need me to, I can always install runway lights in case you get lost going to the bathroom."

I try not to roll my eyes. Like… I *really* try, but I can't help the motion. "Gee, thanks."

The corner of his mouth turns slightly, but it comes across as more of a smirk than a smile. Heat flames through my face. If he weren't so utterly predictable, maybe I wouldn't mind some of the looks he gives. But I know they're just a sign he's trying to come up with his next jab.

*Silly city girl.*

"See you tomorrow," Asher replies, his eyes dragging away from mine.

I watch him disappear around the corner, boots thumping loudly against the hardwood floors. What a grump. I can only imagine what our riding lessons are going to be like.

With a huff, I turn back to the door of my childhood and twist the knob, slowly inching it open as though there's a monster on the other side. A heavy weight settles on my chest when I don't feel even a shard of recollection as I cross the threshold. It's not the happy reunion I had hoped for.

Nothing is familiar, and my mind feels so... blank.

The soft lilac comforter and white quilted pillowcases on my bed don't jog my memory, and the fluffy, cream-colored rug between my toes doesn't bring back any warm feelings of nostalgia either. I don't even recognize the posters of country and pop stars that paint the walls around me. It's just a room full of stuff.

I pick up the small picture frame on my dresser and frown as a lump rises in my throat. It's a photo of a much younger and happier version of myself. The picture was taken somewhere in the mountains. My dad is standing in the middle with one arm around a woman—my mother, I presume—and the other holding me, barefoot and smiling, minus a few front teeth. We're *all* smiling like everything is right in the world. Like everything is as it should be.

But it's not.

I lay the frame, face down, on the corner of my nightstand and look around at the one space in the world that should bring me peace and comfort. I thought coming here would help me find myself, but I feel more lost now than ever.

Tears stream down my face, and I fall into bed, stifling my sobs with a pillow until sleep finally comes.

# Chapter Two

**Asher**

It's early, and my boots pick up drops of morning dew as I cross the field to Mr. Carter's house. I take another swig of coffee from my travel mug and think about the chance he took on me a few years ago when I first moved to Texas and desperately needed to get my life back on track. I owe him a lot for everything he's done for me.

But as much as I owe him, I'm not thrilled he tasked me with being the one to give his estranged daughter riding lessons. Mr. Carter says we just need to jog her memory since she already knows how, but it's still another box to add to my extensive to-do list. And how do we know she can even be trusted? I've met women like her back in Nashville. Even if she did lose her memory, word around town is that she left after high school and never even bothered to call or write. Henry is a good man, and thanks to him, I have steady work and a place to live. The last thing I need is some high-on-her-horse city girl coming around and making waves for me because she has her daddy wrapped around her little finger.

Henry's truck is gone, which means he's already left for town. He likes going to the cafe when they open and getting coffee with the older crowd of town locals. He's probably telling everyone how his pride and joy has finally returned home from the big city. I've never seen the man run as fast as he did when he got the call that Gemma was in an accident. When he returned home with her, something told me that a lot would change.

As I near the house, I'm a bit irritated she's not waiting on the porch ready to go. I was clear about what time our lesson was this morning, but I figured she was probably inside finishing breakfast or mulling over what to wear since Henry had only brought in two suitcases for her.

I open the front door and head toward the kitchen. The house is so quiet you could hear a pin drop. Yep. She's definitely mulling over what to wear. I pass the bathroom on my way down the hall, but there's still no sign of life. Feeling my blood pressure rise, I stop at her bedroom door, knock a few times, then listen. I hear a groan. "Gemma, time to get up. Lessons start now."

Another groan.

Maybe she's used to not being on anyone else's time, but I have a laundry list of chores to do before Mr. Carter gets home, and I'm not in the mood to sit around and wait while she gets her beauty sleep. I push open her door to find her buried under a pile of purple with one arm hanging out over the side of the bed.

"Gemma."

Gemma's hand disappears under the sheets as I yank them off her.

"Hey!"

"Next time it'll be a bucket of water. Now, come on. I need you up." I ignore her death glare. She can be mad at me all she wants when she's up on her horse. "Let's go. Chop, chop."

When Gemma straightens up, a few loose strands of chestnut hair fall over her intense green eyes, picking up flecks of gold and brown, and I have to look away to keep from staring. "Geez. Are you *always* this bright and chipper in the morning?"

Air puffs out of my nose at her snide tone. "Sorry if I left my red carpet out in the truck. Meet me by the barn in five, and don't be late."

I wait outside impatiently for the woman I swear is going to drive me to drinking. Who knows how long it will take her to learn to mount a horse, much less ride one. I roll up my faded flannel shirt sleeve to check my watch. Seven minutes and forty-eight seconds—she's late.

With a loud thud, the front door slams, and I see Gemma coming down the porch steps toward me. I can't hold back. "What in the world are you wearing?"

She has on a pair of black leggings and a cropped graphic tee, which wouldn't be all that inappropriate—I mean... she's got a body to pull off—what does she think she's gonna accomplish? Her sneakers are so clean and white you'd think they were fresh out of the box. I hope she doesn't think they're going to stay that way.

Gemma screws her face up at me. "Clothes that I'm fine with getting dirty."

"Dirty? You think we're rolling around in the mud or something? I'm just showing you how to get on a horse, princess."

Gemma throws her hands up. "This is all I have!"

"Alright, alright. Come on," I say, trying to fight back a smile. She follows me to the stable where Henry's four horses eat hay from their troughs, and I show her the only palomino quarter horse of the bunch. "Your dad told me to pair you with Sunshine. I guess she's who you used to ride when you competed in Junior barrel racing."

"I... competed." Gemma looks surprised, and her words come out more like a statement than a question.

"Guess you were pretty good. Let's see if that sticks." I walk into Sunshine's stall and put on her gear, smoothing my hand along the side of her neck before leading her out to Gemma.

Gemma freezes up, and Sunshine rears back.

"If you're gonna ride her, you have to relax. Let her get used to you." I take Gemma's hand and cautiously place it on Sunshine's neck.

Sunshine relaxes, then leans closer to Gemma's face and blows air out of her nose.

Gemma flinches. "What's she doing?"

I tip my hat up and watch Sunshine's reactions like a hawk. "I think she remembers you."

Gemma stares at Sunshine for a few seconds in silence, her hand still moving along the horse's neck. Her forehead creases like she's deep in thought. Then, a disappointed sigh breaks from her as she looks up at me. "What now?"

It's the first time since Gemma's been home that I've felt sorry for her. I can't imagine how frustrating it is not remembering someone or something that remembers you. "Grab that mounting block and follow me."

I lead Sunshine out of the stable, and Gemma grunts as she picks up the wooden mounting block, hauling it outside behind us.

I glance over my shoulder and smirk as she sets the block down and hastily wipes her hands on her leggings, leaving a trail of red dirt. "Need help?"

"No." Her voice comes out in a bite as she carries the mounting block the rest of the way. Placing it by Sunshine's left side, she looks up at me with a determined yet defiant look.

Something unexpected hits me square in the chest as our eyes lock. Despite her ornery attitude, she might be the most attractive woman I've ever laid eyes on. It's a fleeting thought, but one that lingers just long enough to burn itself into the back of my mind.

When it comes to members of the opposite sex, dating is at the rock bottom of my list of interests. I haven't so much as looked at another woman since my ex-fiancé decided to pack her bags and leave me and Nashville behind three years ago. To say it sparked some trust issues for me moving forward is an understatement.

"Step up here." I motion to the top of the block.

Gemma positions herself and furrows her brows as her hands sweep across the saddle. Placing her hands around the horn, she starts to grip like she's ready to haul herself over until I stop her.

"She's not going to like that."

Gemma gives a pout and pink creeps into her cheeks. Looks like someone doesn't like being told she's wrong.

"You've got a perfectly good stirrup right here," I say, moving to adjust the length on both sides so they are fitted to her.

Gemma flashes me a glare. "Are you going to guide me like a teacher or lecture me like a parent?"

She makes a valid point. My dad voice *did* come out, and maybe I could stand to do a better job instructing her. I half keep expecting her muscle memory to kick in. Or perhaps it's wishful thinking, and I want her to remember so I can get on with my day. Either way, I opt to lower my tone and take a more gentle approach. "Grab the reins with your left hand to control her head and line up your shoulder with hers. Left foot in the stirrup. Right hand on the horn. Push off and swing your right leg over her back. Make sure you clear the cantle—that's the raised part on the back of the saddle—and come down gently."

Gemma nods and braces herself, gripping and launching off the mounting block. She throws her leg over, barely clearing the cantle, and sways out of balance before easing herself into the saddle. Her face brightens as she gets settled.

"There you go." I step back and watch Gemma adjust her feet in the stirrups, placing them just right, almost like instinct. "Now, let's get her to walk. Squeeze her sides with your legs."

Gemma nods and grips the reins, tightening her legs around Sunshine until they begin moving forward. Gemma's mouth curls into a smile, and she sits up straight, holding a posture I can't argue with.

"You look like a natural," I say, walking alongside to keep a close eye on Sunshine. The last thing I need is her going rogue and bucking off the boss's daughter.

Gemma looks down with challenging eyes. "Is that another attempt at sarcasm, or are you being serious?" I like the sass in her voice, but I can tell there's genuine curiosity behind her words. I guess I'd have a hard time believing it, too, if I were in her shoes. "I don't gain anything by lying to you."

She seems satisfied enough by my answer and nods. Sunshine slows her gait, coming to a complete stop, and Gemma leans forward to run her fingers through the soft mane. "I just don't understand. *None* of this feels familiar."

"It will take more than one lesson to see results, Gemma."

She frowns. "But... what if it doesn't work."

I step closer, prompting Gemma's eyes to shift to mine. "If you don't believe it'll work, it won't. We work hard here. And we try hard, too. So, you need to decide how hard you're willing to fight for it."

Gemma purses her lips and holds my gaze momentarily before shaking the tension out of her shoulders. "Okay. So, what now?"

She's determined. I'll give her that.

"Take her for a few laps around the arena. Use your legs and the reins to guide her."

I stand to the side and lean against the rails, watching Gemma ride in circles. I can tell Sunshine is getting restless. After they return from their final lap, I take the reins and guide Sunshine back to the center of the ring. "That'll be good enough for today."

"Good *enough?*" Gemma scoffs. "I mounted her on the first try. And I did my laps—."

"And now, it's time for a break." I step back and motion to a safe area on the ground to land. "Go on."

Gemma wrinkles her nose and shifts awkwardly in her saddle.

"Remember, start with your right leg this time."

"I got it."

Gemma's reply is sharp and biting, and for someone who has no clue what she's doing, she sure isn't doing herself any favors by not listening. I know I shouldn't let her go by herself, but there's something oddly satisfying about watching her try.

White-knuckling the saddle horn, her face is flushed by the time she finally gets her leg over. I watch with satisfaction as she clumsily hangs off Sunshine's side, but my reflexes kick in when she loses her footing in the stirrup.

I jump forward and catch her as she falls back, my arms wrapping around her and guiding her to the ground. "Hold on. I got you."

Gemma grabs my arms in an iron grip, only relaxing when her feet touch the ground. Prying herself away, she whips around and glares at me with fire in her cheek and nostrils flared, and I swear she resembles a bull ready to attack—only I'm not the matador. I'm the red cape about to get mauled.

"Whoa, I offered to help," I say, holding my hands up in defense. "It's not my fault you can't handle a little constructive criticism." She narrows her eyes, and I narrow mine right back this time.

"I don't know what your deal is, but you're literally the worst teacher my dad could've picked! Cop a feel much?" Gemma bites out the words.

"Oh, don't flatter yourself. And trust me, princess, I wasn't dying to be your dad's first choice." The tension between us grows thick, and heat flares through every pore as we face off until we're interrupted by a car approaching.

I tear my eyes away from Gemma to see a familiar white Toyota Highlander rolling up the drive. "Lessons are done for the day."

Before Gemma can speak, I take Sunshine's reins and lead her toward the car. Samantha, a bubbly brunette in her mid-thirties, steps out of the driver's side. I lift my arm to greet her just as the back passenger side door flies open, and a little girl with blonde pigtails and her daddy's blue eyes hops out.

"Daddy!"

I let go of Sunshine's reins and kneel as Hazel throws herself into my arms. She nearly puts me into a chokehold, wrapping her arms around my neck in a tight hug. "Hey, Sweetpea. Did you and Sam have fun at the park this morning?"

Hazel beams and nods. She pulls away and digs into the pocket of her pink shorts, pulling out a weird-shaped rock. "Look what I found!"

I take the small rock and inspect it with a serious expression. "Kind of looks like a funny-looking pumpkin."

"It looks like a cloud!" Hazel laughs as she takes the rock back and stuffs it in her pocket—no doubt to add it to her collection of other weird and wonderful finds.

I scoop her up as I stand, resting her on my hip as Samantha approaches us. "Thanks for taking her this morning. How was she?"

"An angel, as usual. I promised I'd take her to the donut shop tomorrow for breakfast." Samantha says, smiling up at Hazel and giving her a wink. "See you later, alligator."

"In a while, crocodile." Hazel waves goodbye as her nanny of two years gets in her car and heads back down the drive.

Because I'm so busy with chores around the ranch early in the morning, it helps that she's willing to pick Hazel and watch her until I'm finished. Hazel is only six, and getting everything done without worrying about her getting into trouble is difficult.

"What do you say we take Sunshine back to the stable? Then, we can eat some ice cream." I carry Hazel as I lead Sunshine back to the stable.

As we walk back to the guest house, a sudden tug on my brain prompts me to glance over my shoulder. Gemma is standing right where I left her, in the middle of the riding arena, with a dumbfounded look on her face. I never told her I was a single dad, but it's not like we were shooting to be buddies. I'm her instructor. At least, until she pitches a fit to her dad and gets some other poor sap to handle her skyscraper-sized attitude.

Good riddance.

# Chapter Three

**Gemma**

"Alright, lunch is served!"

I raise an eyebrow and lean back in my chair as Dad sets a plate of something deep-fried and drowning in what looks like gravy in front of me. I pick up my fork and poke at it. "What is this?"

"Chicken fried steak. It was one of your favorites." He takes the seat across from me at the wooden dining table and stares with an eager look. All afternoon, he's been introducing me to things from my past, like old pictures and school awards. And I guess, now, he's moving on to favorite foods.

I'd be lying if I said it wasn't overwhelming at times. He always looks at me with this hopeful glint, like he's waiting for my memories to come flooding back every time he shows me something new. Then, I'm forced to politely smile and shake my head... because nothing has felt familiar enough to excite me so far.

More and more, it's crushing me, but I keep my feelings to myself. I know he's just trying to help, so the least I can do is try. And speaking of trying, it's also why I'm still enduring lessons from Asher.

Hearing him make snide 'city girl' jabs all day is like listening to nails on a chalkboard. Could his attitude be any more stony? It blows my mind that he's a single dad. Wolves might as well raise that poor girl. I keep trying to put all the pieces together to figure him out, but nothing fits. Not that it matters. I have my own puzzle to solve, and I can't be distracted every time he throws me a curve ball.

Dad says lunch is chicken fried steak, but I need help wrapping my head around the idea. Who would fry a perfectly good steak? I carefully cut into it, swiping an extra dollop of gravy on top before taking a bite. I half expected something bland, but instead, I'm hit with a rush of flavor that almost seems too greasy and too rich to constitute going back for more, but after my third bite, I'm convinced I've died and gone to heaven. "Oh my gosh." I throw my head back and moan.

"You don't like it?"

"No!" I manage to protest through a mouth full of food. "It's soooo good!" I take a swig of milk and wash it down.

Dad grins. "See? I knew you'd love it. My gravy isn't as good as your maw's, but with a little more bacon grease and black pepper, I think it would make her proud."

We continue eating, and a peaceful silence fills the room before we're interrupted by a loud knock and the sound of the front door swinging open. As quickly as I can stuff a fork full of steak dunked in gravy and mashed potatoes into my mouth, I hear a familiar pair of boots hitting the wood floors, and Asher appears in the entryway. He leans against the door frame, and our eyes lock. Afraid to move a muscle, I seal my lips with cheeks full like a chipmunk.

Charming, Gemma. *Very* charming.

Asher looks at me with a smile that makes me want to crawl into a hole and die. "I finished securing all the fences early, and Sam took Hazel for the day," he says, shifting his focus to my dad. "Anything else you'd like me to do, Sir?"

Dad laces his fingers behind his head and leans back in his chair. "You know what? You should take Gemma into town and help her pick out some riding gear. Weren't you saying you need a new pair of shoes?" He gives me an expectant look. "I bet Asher's just the man to help you pick a pair of sturdy riding boots. He can probably help you find a good pair of britches, too."

I can feel my eyes widen, and I swallow hard, my esophagus burning as the unchewed lump of chicken fried steak works its way down. My father's amusement at his suggestion radiates throughout the room, and I regret opening my big mouth earlier. All it took was a comment in passing about having to scrub dirt off my shoes and feeling like my leggings were too thin for long rides in the saddle, and now he's pawning me off with Satan's spawn—as *if* I need wardrobe advice from a man who, himself, falls victim to fashion. Or the lack thereof.

"I just didn't bring a lot of clothes," I say, trying to maintain my last shred of dignity. "I can go into town by myself. Asher doesn't need to trouble himself."

I see Asher start to nod in agreement out of the corner of my eye, but Dad shakes his head. "Hogwash! I don't want you going around town by yourself, Gemma. Asher knows where to go, and I'm sure it's no trouble at all."

Dad glances at Asher, and then Asher glances at me and shrugs. I guess he can't say no to my father any more than I can.

I lean back and look at the lunch I was so excited to finish before we were so rudely interrupted, and Dad takes my plate and wraps it up with a piece of foil.

"Ready when you are," I say, looking up at Asher and reflecting on my recent run of bad luck. It's bad enough I get slapped with amnesia and have to endure riding lessons with such an insufferable human being. But now my father is insisting he take me clothes shopping? While we're at it, maybe later we can braid each other's hair, too.

I follow Asher to his shiny new Dodge truck, and to my surprise, he gets my door for me.

My arm brushes his as I move past, and I catch the clean scent of leather and tobacco on his skin. The smell is intoxicating and makes me want to bury my face in his shirt. At least now I know he showers.

If only he had the attitude to match, maybe he wouldn't still be single.

I climb inside and buckle up, glancing around to see a tube of sunscreen on the floor, some sunglasses on the dash, and a few rocks in the cup holder. My curiosity peaks, but I don't say anything when he gets in and drives us to town, only five minutes away.

The town is tiny. Most of the businesses border one long main street, with small neighborhoods and farmlands littering the outskirts. We slow down near a stretch of road with a small post office next to a cafe and three older men sitting out front on an old weathered bench.

"We'll check out Sugar Style first," Asher says, taking a parking spot on the street just past the cafe. He hops out of his truck and leads me toward a small boutique with a few clothed mannequins posing in the storefront window.

As we enter, a bell dings above the door and racks of brightly colored clothing fill the space. Upbeat country music pours through a mounted speaker but doesn't mask the sound of a cheery voice from the back of the store.

"Welcome to Sugar Style! Be with you in a second!"

One particular rack catches my eye, and I stop to thumb through various collared shirts, some with fringe and others with exciting patterns and designs. They're nothing like the clothes I packed from New York, and I feel a buzz of excitement, wondering how I would look in something so.... Western.

A pop of color in my dreary world wouldn't be the worst thing ever, and there's hardly a boring option in the entire store. I find myself almost in a trance as I float from one rack to the next, my curiosity melding into intrigue as all my worries melt away.

I pick up a pair of white ankle jeans with a heavy, brown leather belt with rhinestone detail and a large silver buckle and hold it against a maroon puff-sleeve blouse, picturing the outfit in my head.

"Can't wear that riding a horse."

I turn and give Asher a pointed look, snapping myself out of my mental fashion show. "Thank you, Captain Obvious. I'm allowed to look, aren't I?"

Asher huffs and shoves his hands in the pockets of his faded blue jeans, complete with holes worn in both knees.

"While we're out, maybe *you* should look for some new clothes," I say, not bothering to hide my annoyance.

Asher scoffs, detecting my critical tone with ease. "You got something to say about my clothes? Sorry if I don't care to parade around sipping lattes in skinny jeans. It must be a real culture shock."

So, we're doing this now. Carefully, I hang the clothes back on their rack and spin on my heel to face him. With less than a foot between us, I poke him in the chest. "You have a ketchup stain on your shirt, and you're going to sit there and complain about *my* fashion taste?"

Asher parts his lips to speak, but the sound of approaching voices and footsteps stops him short as he looks past me.

Following his gaze, I see a young couple around our age approaching with friendly smiles plastered on their faces—until they see me.

"Gemma? Gemma Carter, is that you?" the woman gasps, her blue eyes filling with recognition. With her short, curvy figure and coils of long, copper-colored hair, she doesn't look the least bit familiar to me, even if it's clear she knows me.

"Well, look at what the cat drug in," the man chuckles in disbelief, gawking as his shaggy, dark hair nearly covers his eyes. "I never thought I'd see the day you'd finally decide to come home to Sugar Plum!"

My confusion is so intense that I'm paralyzed as they approach. I have no idea who these people are and why they're saying these things. Why *wouldn't* I come back to my hometown?

Asher seems to notice my discomfort and steps forward to intercept them. "Hold up, you two. She doesn't know who you are."

"What do you mean she doesn't know who I am? *Sure* she does. We've been friends since kindergarten." The woman smiles hopefully, which only adds to my level of unease. I want to smile back, but I don't. This situation is too much to process, and I wish I could run and hide.

"She got into an accident and lost her memories. She's back home to try to get them back," Asher says, prompting shocked looks to fill their faces.

"Oh, man. Gem, that's awful. I'm sorry to hear that." The man gives a look of sympathy that I should probably get used to once word starts spreading around town about my condition.

I'm not ready for that.

"This is Joshua and his girlfriend, Olivia. She owns the boutique."

Asher introduces the couple, and an awkward tension fills the air as the four of us look at each other. It's not an ideal afternoon for my first day out on the town, but all I can do is try to roll with it. Immersion is the best way to get my memories back, right? "Nice to meet you. Or... see you again, I guess."

They offer polite smiles, and Olivia is the first to break the silence. "You look really good! Your hair used to be so long, but short hair suits you. And I love the color. You look like you'd fit right in in the big city."

I reach up and touch the ends of the waves as they barely graze my shoulders—the only length I've ever known. "Oh, thank you. Seems like it'd be easier to maintain."

"Well, once you get a taste of the wind here, you'll wish it was longer. I can't leave the house without a ball cap. Olivia thinks it's long enough to start wearing one of those man buns." Joshua chuckles before glancing over at Asher. "So, what are you two doing together?"

"Mr. Carter has me giving her riding lessons. Says the doctor thinks it'll help jog her memory. Wants me to take her shopping," Asher says. Our eyes briefly meet, and the way he doesn't bother to speak in complete sentences makes my skin prickle. Could he sound any more miserable about being stuck with me all afternoon?

"Oh, that's great! I remember how much you loved your horses," Olivia says, cutting the tension. "Gosh, there's so much to catch you up on. Sugar Plum hasn't been the same without you, girly."

Joshua nods in agreement. "You're going to have a line of people wanting to see you."

I know they mean well with their words, but the pressure of it all drops on my shoulders like an anvil. I feel my chest tighten, and my head starts to throb as I glance around. I feel so small and helpless. I wish I could remember like they want me to.

But I can't.

All of the hope and recognition around me makes me feel like a failure, and I can handle only so much. "I... uh... I'm feeling pretty tired. I should probably head home."

"Yeah, no problem. We'll catch up another time," Olivia says with a smile that almost looks sad.

I look at Asher with pleading eyes only meant for him. So what if he's the same cocky ranch hand that makes a sport out of insulting me. Right now, he's the only one who can save me from myself. "Can you take me home?"

Asher nods without hesitation, relieved, I'm sure, to bring our outing to an abrupt end. After saying goodbye to Joshua and Olivia, he leads me back to his truck without a word.

Peering out the window, I fight back the surge of emotions that threaten to crash down on top of me. I don't know how I can feel so out of touch with my own life. I want to make the most of my time here, but I feel the pressure to remember haunt me as I struggle to piece together the puzzle of my life until the memories finally return.

If they ever do.

# Chapter Four

**Asher**

With a quick flick of the wrist, I cast my line out and watch the bobber meet the surface as Joshua and I troll the lake in his Jon boat. After adjusting the drag, I slide the end of the rod into a makeshift pole holder and sink into the chair beside him.

"So, how's it going with Gemma? Any luck on the memory front?" Joshua says, keeping his eyes fixed on the water as he makes another cast.

I shake my head. "No. Nothing yet. She's finally getting into a routine, though. Mr. Carter thinks that might help. But she's got a long road ahead of her, and who knows what will or won't help at this point. He's trying everything—photos, stories, home videos—but nothing rings a bell for her."

Joshua gives a troubled nod. "I can't imagine how she must feel right now. If my memories went poof, I'd lose it."

I think about the confusion and sadness I see in her eyes and how quiet she gets when too many people are around the house, and a wave of guilt washes over me when I think about all the times I try to get a rise out of her. It's all fun and games until I catch glimpses of her sitting alone on the front porch, void of emotion.

The only time I've ever seen a spark of passion in her eyes is during our lessons. She becomes alive, even if it's to argue with me or make some sharp comment. I think it's because she knows there's no pressure to remember things from the past. After all, I didn't know her back then. There's nothing for me to compare her to. Maybe she finds some solace in that.

"Yeah, I'm sure it's hard. She's tough as nails, though," I reply.

Joshua chuckles. "She's always been a force to reckon with, but she wears her heart on her sleeve, too. It used to get her in trouble back in high school with some of the guys she dated. She was a real sweetheart. The type to always put others before herself. And some people took advantage of her good nature."

Gemma? Sweet? I almost laugh in disbelief.

"What you're doing for her, Ash... helping her, it's really good of you." Joshua continues, deflating any animosity that I currently harbor toward the woman I swear is determined to drive me to an early grave.

Gemma and I may not get along, but I've known from the start I'd need to see this through with her until she gets her memories or gives up altogether. My momma raised me to be helpful and kind, and my values don't differ from one person to the next. I help because it's the right thing to do, even if it's troublesome.

"I'm trying my best, but I don't know enough about her to feel like I can make a difference. What's the last thing you remember of her?"

He hums under his breath for a moment. "Graduation. She left town pretty fast after that. She was chasing her dreams when she took off to start a career in the big city, and nobody's seen her since. Until now."

She made it to the city and never came back—at all? The thought doesn't sit well. I still visit my parents in Nashville for the holidays, even if it brings back the memory of having my heart ripped out. And having to tell Hazel that her mom left and wasn't coming back is a conversation that haunts me to this day.

"There has to be something. Was there anything special that she liked? Or a person? An old boyfriend, maybe that might spark a memory?"

Joshua thinks to himself before perking up. "There's an old apple orchard back behind the ranch she used to love. Every year, she'd bring a basket of apples to homeroom."

I raise a brow, realizing I know which orchard he's talking about. I've passed through there a few times with Hazel, always putting her on my shoulders so she could pick a few to take home and share with Mr. Carter. It would make sense if Gemma were always out there. It's only a few miles from the house, and I've been told the property belongs to an old family friend. "Noted. Thanks."

He smiles and gives a nod. "And if she's up for it, tell her to swing by the shop. Olivia would be happy to help if she still wants to pick out some new clothes."

"Thanks. I'll let her know."

Gemma got pretty overwhelmed after the last time. I don't know if she'll want to brave another trip to town any time soon, but she can't hide out at the ranch forever. This is her hometown, which means her memories are strung up all over. And if she's not ready to face the crowds, I know just the place to take her.

I'm snapped out of my thoughts by a bend in the tip of my rod, and I look out to see my bobber disappear below the surface as my reel begins to click with a vengeance. My heart pounds as I snatch up the rod to give it a good jerk, and like music to my ears, the line starts whizzing.

"Fish on!" I plant my feet and begin the fight back and forth, seeing an impressive largemouth on the other end of the line jump before it reaches the boat. "You got the net?"

Joshua leans forward and helps me bring the bass into the boat, freeing the hook and giving me a nudge. "There you go, boy!" Moving fast, he pulls a tape measure out of his tackle box and checks the size. "Bro, fifteen and a half inches! She's a keeper."

"Put it on ice, then one more cast. I've got riding lessons in an hour." My thoughts shift to Gemma and her reaction when I tell her we'll be changing it up today. She already made a fuss about another early morning lesson, so I agreed to push it back to late afternoon so we could be back just before supper time.

"You got it. Maybe today will be the day, right?" he says as he kicks open the cooler and tosses the fish in.

"The day for what?"

He slams the cooler shut and uses the front of his jeans to wipe slime from his hands. "The day she'll get her memories back."

I weigh the odds. Everyone is so hopeful that Gemma will remember everything, but amnesia is unpredictable, especially the kind Mr. Carter says she has. According to the doctors, nothing's a guarantee. "Maybe. We'll see."

After helping Joshua load his boat onto the trailer, we say our goodbyes, and I head back to my truck with a cooler and the only catch of the day. Hazel won't touch seafood, but Mr. Carter loves it when I bring home fresh fish.

I return to the ranch with two minutes to spare and find Gemma waiting for me by the stable. "Is your dad around?"

Gemma walks over to me, shaking her head. When she gets close, she recoils and makes a gagging sound before covering her nose. "No... ughh! What's that smell?"

We were out on the water for so long that I hardly notice. "Fish, I'm guessing. I have a largemouth bass he can take. I'll just keep it on ice until he gets back."

"Aren't you going to shower or change clothes, at least?" Gemma asks, taking a few steps back.

"Are you always going to be this dramatic?" She rolls her eyes. "Fine. Give me ten minutes, and I'll meet you back here."

Not wanting to hear her gripe and moan for the next hour and a half, I head back to the house and hop in the shower to scrub away the smell of victory. After buttoning up a dark green flannel, I pull on a pair of work jeans, making sure they're free of holes, then slip into my boots and spritz my chest with a dab of cologne for good measure. I wouldn't want to offend any more of her delicate senses.

When I meet her outside, I see she's already brought Sunshine out of her stall and walk over to inspect her handiwork.

"Yes, I positioned the saddle correctly." Gemma's words are sharp, and I can tell her guard is up immediately.

I don't smile but give my nod of approval. She may not always be on time, but at least she pays attention to details. "Looks good to me."

She looks surprised. "Wow. That's a first. I figured you'd at least find *something* to criticize," she says, planting her hands on her hips. I can tell she's chomping at the bit for me to challenge her.

"Looks like you're finally starting to pay attention during lessons."

Gemma's jaw tenses briefly, but she dismissively waves her hand at whatever thoughts she must have. "So, what are we doing today? More laps around the field?"

"No." I shake my head and turn to the stable. "We're taking a field trip. I'll grab Scout, and then we'll be on our way."

"Whoa, wait a minute!" Gemma protests, and I can feel her hot on my heels. "On our way where? We're leaving the property?"

"Just hold on now. You'll see soon enough." Feeling amused by her theatrics, I disappear to retrieve Scout, a sorrel-colored quarter horse, from his stall. He's my go-to any time I ride, but his neighbors, Angel and Jasper, are dependable horses, too. "Maybe next time, guys," I whisper.

Once I get his gear on, I pull myself into the saddle and lead him back out to Gemma, who's already mounted and wearing a troubled look on her face. "Don't look so nervous. You can trust me."

Gemma laughs. "Oh, really?"

"Really," I say, looking so deep into her eyes I almost lose myself.

We steer the horses north, putting the ranch far behind until we finally see the line of trees I'm looking for in the distance. I take a quick glance at Gemma and note her casual riding posture. She's a natural, alright. It makes me wonder if anything will be left to teach her after today. But I know these lessons are about more than just teaching her how to ride.

"We're a long way from home. You know, taking a helpless woman out into the woods miles from civilization might constitute some alarm."

I let out a dry laugh. "I've seen what your daddy keeps locked up in the shed. That ain't a man to mess with."

"Oh, come on. My dad wouldn't hurt a fly."

"In his eyes, you'll always be his little girl, Gemma. He might be soft when you're around, but there's nothing he wouldn't do to protect his own. I picked that up the day I met him. It's been an honor learning from a man like that."

"And now you're saddled with me for being such a good right-hand man."

"Yeah. Doesn't seem like much of a reward, now that I think about it." Gemma swats in my direction as we close in on the field of trees. "Calm down, now. Wouldn't want to fall off your high horse. I brought you out here to show you something."

"Show me what?" Gemma says, steering Sunshine close behind.

"Look." I point to the rows of trees ripe with crisp apples and stop to watch her eyes sweep over the sea of pink and green.

Her eyes go wide in a flash, and her lips part in a gasp.

My heart stops as a single thought crosses my mind.

She remembers.

# Chapter Five

**Gemma**

I can't believe my eyes. I look around the orchard, taking in the pinkish hue of the apples and the fullness of the leaves. I can't believe I'm here!

"It's so... beautiful. I've never seen anything quite like it," I breathe out.

Asher's shocked expression plummets off his face. "Wait, what? You don't remember this place?"

I turn to him, a bit confused. "No, am I supposed to?"

He sighs, and his expression goes sullen, which makes my chest ache. There's that disappointment I see so much. "Word around town is that you really liked this place back in the day. For a minute there, I thought you might have remembered it."

I look away and shake my head. "Sorry. I wish I did, though. It seems like a really special place."

"Yeah, it is. Sometimes, I take Hazel out here to pick apples."

He motions for me to follow him, and the weight on my chest feels a little less heavy as he leads us deeper into the orchard. I like it when he talks about his daughter. Then again, I like it when he talks about *anything* I'm not expected to know already. Just being here and knowing it was a place I knew well makes me feel stuck in a past I can't remember. It's nice hearing about someone else's life for a change.

"That's a good memory for her to have," I say, not realizing the irony of my words until they leave my mouth.

We look at each other for a long moment, and at first, Asher doesn't say anything. The tension that lingers between us is almost palpable. Another moment passes, and I can't stop the pitiful look that washes over my face.

Asher chuckles light-heartedly and shakes his head. "Sorry. I shouldn't laugh."

"It's okay," I assure him. And it is. Being here with him, riding horses while sunlight still shines through the trees, fills my stomach with a radiating warmth that helps calm my nerves. "I can see why I used to love coming here, too. It's peaceful."

"It's another half hour to sunset. We can stay until then if you'd like."

"Oh, no. I'm sure you have better things to do than babysit me. Besides, don't you have to get back to Hazel?"

Asher hums under his breath as he dismounts, his brown cowboy boots hitting the ground with a thud. "Nope. Not today. She's at a sleepover with Sam and her niece."

Before I have time to protest, he's by my side, offering a hand for support. I look down at it for a second before finally caving and giving it a firm grip. Carefully, I swing my leg over and perch on the saddle, trying to figure out how to hop off without twisting an ankle. Parts of my body are still recovering from the injuries I sustained back in New York, and I'd rather not tack on any new ones.

"Well, it would help if you weren't facing the wrong way. You're gonna fall flat on your face if you try to jump down like that," Asher laughs. "Hold on."

Suddenly, his hands are on my waist, and he's hoisting me off the saddle, lowering me down to the ground with controlled ease like I'm a feather.

My face burns, but I manage a grateful nod. "Thanks. I guess I need a little more practice with my dismount."

"You'll get the hang of it," Asher replies, stepping away to tie Scout and Sunshine to a few trees nearby.

My eyes fix on his broad back and slowly trail south, making a mental note of just how well he's wearing those Wranglers. And the way his sleeves grip his biceps makes my knees feel weak. Of course, I'd never admit it to his face, but he sure is one fine specimen of man.

"You coming?"

I scold myself for getting distracted and follow him through the rows of trees, admiring the stark contrast of colors. Yellows and pinks popping on a waxy green canvas. The orchard must be several acres in size, and the more time we spend walking around, the more clouds gather in the sky above us. "Is it just me, or are those clouds looking pretty dark?"

Asher tilts back his head and peers up through the canopies. "Yeah, a little. Shouldn't rain, though. I checked the weather this morning."

"The best way to check the weather is to look up," I reply dryly, not liking the sudden overcast or the fact that we've ventured so far away from the ranch. Not to mention the fact we must be clear on the other side of the orchard at this point.

Asher doesn't look amused. "Alright, let's head back. Last thing we need is to get caught in the rain in the dark."

We turn and start back in the direction we came, and a cool breeze coasts through the air, making the hairs on the back of my arm stand up—a storm breeze. We barely make it to the horses before a flash of lightning appears in the distance, followed by a rumble of thunder and fat drops of rain that hit me square in the face.

"Uh oh." That's all I can get out before the wind picks up and we're met with a downpour. Leaves rattle all around but offer no shelter. We both cower to avoid getting wet while he unties the horses, but it's useless. I put my hands above my head and whip around to face him. "What do we do?"

Asher looks in two different directions—south, where we rode in from, and to the east. "Lead Sunshine by the reins. Follow me!"

My jaw nearly drops as he grabs Scout's reins and starts jogging away from the ranch. The roar of rain and thunder is so loud that even if I yelled to ask where on Earth he thinks he's going, I doubt he'd hear me.

"Come on, Sunshine," I say, grabbing the reins and rushing to catch up.

The grass is soaking wet, creating a squelching sound every time my tennis shoes make contact, and I curse myself for not going back into town for a new pair of boots when I almost lose my footing a few times on slippery grass. After picking up the pace, I can squint and make out the silhouettes of Asher and Scout through the trees up ahead.

"Gemma, this way! Hurry!"

So bossy! "I'm right behind you!"

I glance back at Sunshine, who has no problem keeping up, and speed up even more when I feel my clothes and hair grow heavy with moisture. Coldness seeps over my skin, but a flicker of hope erupts when I see an old barn looming ahead.

Asher leads Scout through a large open door and runs his fingers through his thick black hair, smoothing back the soaked strands. He turns to pull the door shut just as I make it inside, and instantly, I'm hit with the smell of dust and old hay.

"I know it looks rough, but we'll be safe here until it passes. Sorry, I got you into this mess."

I glance around at the interior of the dilapidated two-story building, noting the alarming number of cobwebs and old, rotting wood. I can see where the horse stalls used to be, as well as a few other pens, which are nearly falling apart. I wouldn't be surprised if a strong gust of wind was enough to take the whole thing down. "How did you even know about this place?"

"I found it one day when I was out riding." I try not to stare as Asher unbuttons his flannel shirt and takes it off to wring water from the bottom of the white tank top underneath. "I asked your dad about it, and he said it's been abandoned ever since the new owner took over the orchard. It's sitting on public land, though. Don't have to worry about some grumpy cowboy showing up to kick us out."

"And here I thought I was with the only grumpy cowboy in Sugar Plum," I say, feeling a buzz of amusement. I'm still cold and wet, but at least we're out of the rain. Silver linings, right?

Asher raises a brow as a smile pulls at the corner of his mouth. "I could've left you out in the rain, you know."

I narrow my eyes. "You wouldn't."

"Try me."

I want to come back with some intelligent, playful remark, but I'm tired. It's all I can do to roll my eyes before glancing around again, this time searching for a place to get comfortable. From the sound of the rain outside, we may be stuck here for a while.

"We should probably call my father and let him know we're safe since we won't be back in time for dinner."

Asher nods and fishes his phone out of his back pocket. He frowns. Determined, he lifts it in the air and walks around the barn, looking up at it like it's about to reveal the winning lottery numbers. After hitting all four corners, his shoulders slump forward, and he mutters, "No service."

"Shocker."

Asher sighs and pockets his phone. "Your dad's gonna worry if we're not home soon."

"What else are we going to do? Ride through the rain?" I can imagine him worrying, but I know he trusts Asher. Maybe Asher could get us home safe if we left now, but the thought of staying dry clouds my better judgment.

Asher shrugs as his eyes drift over to Scout. He's not seriously considering it....*is he?*

I flash him a sharp look. "Absolutely not."

He looks back at me, and I swear I see an evil grin creep across his face.

"No! We are staying right here until that storm is over. I don't care how long it takes." In protest, I plop down on the ground, not caring about the absurd amount of hay now stuck to the back of my favorite pair of jogger pants. At least it's dry.

"As you wish, princess."

My face burns, but a shiver runs through my limbs, prompting me to rub my arms as they flare with goosebumps. I can still feel the wind from the storm blowing through the open door, and it doesn't help that my clothes are still cold and wet.

Asher's smirk shifts to a look of concern, and he frowns slightly before turning to dig through his saddlebag, pulling out a lighter and a small orange pouch. He wanders around for a minute or two as though taking a mental inventory, then disappears into a dark corner without a word.

With the door closed, there's not much light to see much of anything, and I have to shake the eerie feeling I get after a few minutes pass with no sign of Asher. "Asher...?" I try to steady my shaky voice. "If you're playing a joke, it isn't funny."

Just before my eyes have time to start playing tricks on me, Asher emerges from the shadows with a handful of weathered wood scraps and an entertained look on his face. "Don't tell me you're getting scared now."

I let out a quiet sigh of relief at the sight of him. He may be my nemesis, but if he gets taken down by some creepy shadow dweller, I'm toast.

"Trust me, if there were anything even remotely threatening, you'd scare it away with that sorry sense of humor."

Asher rolls his eyes as he arranges the planks of wood into an empty, round feeding trough, tossing a few handfuls of straw into the bottom before lighting them on fire. He leans back as the flames spread and pulls the orange pouch from his pocket to reveal a shiny, thin metallic blanket that he unfolds and wraps around my shoulders. "There. Now, let's get you warm."

As if in a trance, my eyes settle on him as he takes the spot on the hay beside me and leans back, studying the flames as they dance. Why is he being so nice all of a sudden? Did some alien cockroach crawl into his ear while he was getting wood and take over his body? Or maybe he hit his head, and now he has amnesia like me. I cringe at the latter thought.

As he leans back on one hand, shadows flicker across his face, and I tear my eyes away to lose myself in the fire's trance. Trying to recover memories with amnesia is a slow and uphill battle that has, so far, yielded no results. I don't understand. I'm doing everything the doctor ordered by engaging in old activities, but even the horseback riding lessons aren't working.

Well, okay. So it's not like I've been *completely* focusing on the lessons like I should be. But who could blame me? Focusing on Asher and our complicated dynamic is a full-time job that doesn't pay nearly enough.

Oh, Asher.

I try to focus on the fire and not the fact that he's sitting so close to me. Or that we're actually sharing a moment of peace and quiet. All I know is that if I'm going to remember who I was, I can't be getting distracted by him and his unique brand of Southern charm—if that's what you want to call it.

That means from now on, lessons are strictly for business. If I can remember my horseback riding days, hopefully, my other memories will follow suit. There's simply no time for a man who keeps proving himself to be my number one distraction and my number one thorn in my side.

# Chapter Six

**Asher**

Despite the sounds of crackling fire and rain hammering the roof, the abandoned barn is a bit too quiet for my taste. Don't get me wrong. I don't mind it, but Gemma is never quiet around me. She's *always* got something to say.

I glance at her through the corner of my eye to see her practically mean-mugging the fire. "What's with the face? You mad it's not warm enough or something?"

Gemma pulls herself out of her death stare and shakes her head, pulling her knees up to her chest. "Wish I'd have picked a few apples so we'd have something to eat."

For someone so cranky, she sure is cute when she's not jumping down my throat for something. I stand up and walk over to Scout, digging in my saddle bag for the stainless steel water bottle I always keep on hand and two small packages of animal crackers. "Good thing I came prepared."

"Animal crackers?" Gemma asks, looking amused.

"They're Hazel's favorite." When I hand her the bottle and a pack of crackers, our fingertips briefly graze before I draw away and reposition myself on the floor.

Gemma nods and lifts a subtle brow. "You know, I was surprised to find out you had a daughter."

"That doesn't surprise me," I reply. I saw the look on her face when she first saw Hazel. "I don't tend to blast my business to strangers."

Gemma scoffs. "That's smart. And probably for the best, seeing as I don't know myself well enough to know you can trust me."

I crack a smile, and we share a smile. At least she can laugh a little about her situation. I can't imagine anyone having to go through what she has. "Hazel's all I've got these days. She's my whole world. Don't know who I'd be without her."

"She seems like such a happy girl. I keep seeing her running around and chasing the chickens, but I haven't tried talking to her. I know how protective you must be. I don't want to overstep any boundaries."

I have to hide a look of surprise. Considerate isn't a hat I've seen Gemma wear yet. "Wouldn't mind if you did. She'll chat your ear off, though. Consider yourself warned."

"Good. It'd be a welcomed distraction from all the chatter going on in my mind."

The atmosphere around us grows a degree heavier. I can feel the weight on my chest and shoulders, and I can't even imagine how heavy it must feel for her. "That bad, huh?"

Gemma nods after a moment, our eyes locking. There's more vulnerability in them than she'd probably ever admit, but she doesn't let me look into them for long. She lets the emergency blanket fall off her shoulders onto the floor and inches closer to the heat. "Sorry, pal. Like it or not, *you're* the one who gets to talk my ear off tonight. Since we're stuck here, and all."

"In case you haven't noticed, I'm not a big talker." I shrug, unsure of what else I'd say even if I was. I surround myself with a select few I care about, work hard, and avoid drama at all costs. That about sums it up for me.

"Come on. Tell me something I don't already know about you. Something other than the fact that you're a single dad who works on a ranch."

I pop another animal cracker in my mouth, chewing slowly as I contemplate how much more I want to share. "Alright. I'm a traveling rodeo cowboy when I'm not working for your dad."

Gemma's jaw drops. "No way! You're a real-life cowboy?"

It's all I can do not to throw my head back and laugh. "You sound like being a cowboy makes me some mystical creature. I hate to be the bearer of bad news, but my kind make up the majority here. Welcome to West Texas, sweetheart."

Gemma crosses her arms over her chest, looking unamused. "So, what exactly is it that a traveling rodeo cowboy does?"

"Well, I—" I part my lips to speak but see a small crumb near the corner of her mouth.

"What?"

"You've got something... here." I reach out, but Gemma cuts me off. Frowning, she brushes her fingertips against her mouth, missing the crumb entirely.

I shake my head. "Almost."

Gemma huffs a frustrated sigh and tries again, nudging the crumb down toward her bottom lip, but it keeps getting caught in her lip gloss.

"Hold on," I reach out and gently brush away the tiny crumb, my fingertip grazing her bottom lip.

When I pull my hand away, our eyes draw together like magnets.

"Thanks." She finally breaks away and takes a long pull from the water bottle, setting it beside her after she screws the cap back on. "Now, stop stalling and answer my question."

"I ride bulls."

"Bulls? That's crazy! Doesn't it hurt when you get thrown off? What if you break something?"

I shrug. "Sometimes. Hazard of the job, I suppose. You get used to it. And I've broken plenty of bones. Just not enough to keep me out of the saddle."

Gemma's eyes drop to the floor, and there's a long silence. The fire casts shadows across her face, highlighting some of her features. Her curious green eyes. The subtle curve of her nose. The slight curl of her lips. "Sounds like an exciting life. I wish I had more memories to share."

"Just because you don't have any memories doesn't mean there's nothing on your mind. Tell me something about you."

"I'm not sure you want to hear anything that's on my mind right now," Gemma laughs.

I reach around her to pick up the water bottle and take a few swigs before passing it back. "Try me."

Gemma looks away and fixes her eyes on the fire. She shrugs like she's trying to act nonchalant, but I can see the deep furrows forming in her brow. "I don't know. I knew getting my memories back would be hard, but I didn't expect to feel like... such a disappointment."

Her words settle in, and I can't tell if I'm more confused or surprised by them. "Disappointment? Like you're disappointed in yourself?"

She shakes her head. "Like people are disappointed in *me*. I can't remember what they want me to, and I see it in their eyes."

"Now, that's just ridiculous. Nobody is disappointed in you, Gemma. They're disappointed *for* you. People want you to remember for you. Not for them."

"You're probably right. It all feels so much harder than I thought it would be, and nothing I try seems to be working. Some days, I don't even want to get out of bed."

"I know nothing you do guarantees an outcome, but that's no reason to quit showing up. Think of all the new memories you could be making along the way. You can't do that if you're living life cooped up in your room, waiting for the old ones to return.

"So, you're saying I should move on with my life? And forget about the past?"

"I'm not saying that at all. I think you're putting too much pressure on yourself and holding yourself back. I don't want to see you down, but those memories could take a long time to resurface, and that's if they ever do. I know it's not my place, but maybe you should think about the kind of life you want to live if they don't."

Gemma's face relaxes. "No.... You make a valid point. I may never remember my past, but I should make the most of the present while I'm trying. Right?"

The way she searches my eyes for understanding makes me feel like I'm some wise Jedi master and she's my Padawan in training. It's a pleasant shift from the defiant attitude she normally packs around. She may know how to push my buttons, but I could get used to this newfound determination and headstrong will. "I think that'd be a smart thing to do."

Gemma holds my gaze and nods. I watch her eyes narrow and her jaw tense up, almost like she's steadying herself. "Me too. I just need to stay focused."

I nod in agreement, concealing a smile when she yawns. "Why don't you get some sleep? You can use my saddlebag as a pillow. I do it all the time. It's pretty comfortable."

Gemma looks unsure at first, but her eyelids look so heavy they're fluttering. "Maybe just a quick nap. I want to be ready to go in an hour when the rain lets up."

It's hard to tell what the weather will do at this point, but I don't argue. She needs to rest. I hop to my feet, grab my saddle bag, and then drop it down beside her. "I'll wake you when the rain stops."

"Thanks." Gemma's eyes flutter shut as soon as her ear hits the bag, and she's out like a light.

Trying to keep quiet, I tend to the fire, glancing over at her every so often while she sleeps. I'm a little sore with myself for not checking the weather like I said. I'll never admit how distracted I've been since Gemma's been around, but let's just say I've made more than one clumsy mistake thinking about her when I should have been focusing on my work.

When the warmth of the fire finally starts to penetrate, my body finally starts to relax. The sound of heavy rain on the tin roof sends my mind into a trance. The emergency blanket is crumpled under Gemma's shoulder, and I fish it out to lay back on while my flannel hangs to dry.

It doesn't sound like the rain is letting up any time soon when I stretch out next to Gemma thinking I'll just rest my eyes for a few minutes.

That's the last thought that crosses my mind before I drift into a deep sleep.

# Chapter Seven

**Gemma**

I wake with a jolt, and my back feels like it spent the night on a lumpy mattress made of regrets. Note to self: Next time you consider taking a floor nap, kindly remind yourself that discomfort is *not* a personal growth strategy. Rays of sunlight stream in through the cracks in the walls, making me squint. Where *am* I? My mind lags at first, but the memories from last night slowly filter back into my brain. At least the rain stopped.

I turn my head and see Asher passed out on the floor beside me, and if I had a camera, I'd take a picture. His cowboy hat is covering his entire face, and he's on his back stretched out perfectly, legs crossed, and both hands resting on his stomach. He looks so… peaceful. But peace is the last thing on my mind right now.

I scoot away with burning cheeks, trying not to wake him, and bury my face in my hands. I have to suppress my urge to groan in frustration and grind my teeth instead while the conversation from last night plays on repeat in my head.

His intoxicating laugh. His quick wit and captivating sense of humor. His ability to break down some of the walls I've so carefully built around my heart.

I said things out loud I thought I'd never say to anyone—apart from maybe a *really* good therapist. I knew Asher would be trouble from the minute I saw him. I told myself to stay focused. I should know better than to let some country boy charm me out of my better senses. Yet, here we are, spending the night together in a barn in the middle of nowhere. My father is probably worried sick.

"What time is it?"

I nearly jump out of my skin at the sound of Asher's voice as he sits up and rubs the back of his head, and I remember he's the reason we got into this mess.

"So much for waking me up when the storm passed," I mutter hostilely as I get to my feet and start wiping the blanket of dust and hay from my clothes.

"Starting early this morning, huh?" Asher hauls himself off the ground, sounding equally as bitter and resentful.

It feels easier this way—bickering with him and keeping distance between us—and having deep, emotional conversations like the one we had last night *certainly* isn't helping my cause.

Because let's face it. A lost woman with no memories or direction shouldn't have anything to do with a handsome cowboy with a daughter and his life together. At least, not when mine is already so... complicated.

"We need to get back to the ranch." My words come out colder than I intend, and Asher looks almost stung when I brush past him to untie Sunshine.

"Right," he says quietly, gathering the saddlebag and other supplies from the floor. I can feel his eyes on me every so often as we saddle up, which makes my face burn even more.

Alright, Gemma. It's time to put your game face on. No more romantic rides off into the sunset. No more getting vulnerable and sharing your feelings late at night. And *absolutely* no more sleeping next to the enemy. "Ready?" I ask, focusing on petting Sunshine's mane in a last-ditch effort to avoid eye contact.

Any warmth that radiated from him last night is gone, replaced by his usual stony demeanor. He probably thinks I'm mad at him, but I'm not going to correct him and tell him that he's not the one I'm mad at. It's for the best if we pretend last night never happened.

The best for both of us.

Asher doesn't make it easy, though. I've never tried mounting her without my block, and when he sees me try, he's immediately by my side. His hands rest on my waist as I find my footing in the stirrup and steady me... physically, at least.

Hopping off the toes of my right foot, I swing my leg over and slide down into the saddle like it's something I've done a thousand times. A part of me wants to smile and celebrate my victory with Asher, but instead, I give him a curt nod before guiding Sunshine out of the barn.

The grass still glistens from the rain, and humidity lingers as the sun rises. I glance back at the barn one last time, memories from last night flashing in my mind. Maybe sleeping in a barn isn't so terrible, but it reminds me why Asher and I can never be more than... whatever it is we are.

He has the kind of life any man would be jealous of. A well-paying job on the ranch with an exciting career on the side that allows him to pursue his passions. Amazing friends. A beautiful daughter.

And you know what I have? An empty mind and a whole lot of baggage.

In what world does that work?

"This way," Asher says, trotting ahead.

I grip the reins tighter and nudge Sunshine to move faster so we can catch up. The wind blowing through my hair calms my nerves, making me want to stop and enjoy the view. But as much as I want to linger in the apple orchard one last time, we breeze right through it on our way back to the ranch.

I'm not surprised when I see my father standing on the porch with a phone pressed against his ear. He looks so worried. I can only imagine the thoughts he must've had when I never came home. What if he thought I took off back to New York?

When we get closer, the sound of hooves draws his attention. Muttering a few quick words I can't hear, he ends the call and shoves his phone into the back pocket of his work jeans.

"Where in the world have you been? I've been looking for you all night! Calling neighbors. Checking every store in town. Making sure you weren't in a ditch somewhere!" Dad yells as he storms over.

But I quickly realize it's not me he's gunning for. The moment Asher has two boots on the ground, Dad is jabbing a finger into his chest. "What were you thinking taking Gemma off somewhere for the night? You're supposed to be teaching her how to horseback ride to help with her memory loss!"

Asher frowns as my dad rips into him, and doesn't dare to argue. He truly thinks that he's in the wrong.

I'm not so compliant.

With cat-like reflexes, I slide off Sunshine and land without a fall, wedging myself between the two and putting my hands up in defense.

"Dad, it's okay! *I'm* okay. Asher took me to an apple orchard, and we found shelter in an old barn when the storm hit. He wanted to get us back last night, but I was being stubborn. I was scared and didn't want to ride home in the rain. None of this is his fault."

"And you didn't think to call and let me know?" He shoots a look over my shoulder at Asher, but this time, his voice is softer and more concerned than angry.

"I didn't have my phone, but Asher tried to call you. There wasn't any service. I'm so sorry, Daddy."

That last word is all it takes to melt away any residual iciness from my father's glare. He looks at me with hopeful eyes, then returns them to Asher. "You went to the orchard? Did she... remember?" His eyes shift back to mine, and I smile bittersweetly.

"No, Dad. I couldn't remember. But I can see why I used to spend so much time there. I'd like to go again soon if that's okay. I can even bring some apples home for you. Asher told me how much you love them."

The disappointment I feel for being unable to remember eases when his eyes light up. "Of course it is, Peanut. I'd like that. You know, your mom used to make a mean apple pie. I'll see if I can dig up the recipe."

There's a flicker of sadness when he mentions my mom, and I find myself leaning in to wrap my arms around him for our first hug. It's funny. I don't remember my mother at all, but I can feel the magnitude of her past presence as he hugs me back.

Forgotten memories of her are planted everywhere—from an ornamental vase in the living room that Dad says she viciously bid for at a local auction to the red and white potholders in a drawer by the stove and scattered pictures on the walls from all her adventures with Dad and me, she still has so much life in our home.

Home. A word that, despite any chill left in the air from last night's storm, warms me to the bone.

Dad gives one more squeeze before letting go. "I'm gonna run to town now and call off the rescue, but there's leftovers in the fridge. Help yourself to anything that looks good. And oh... Get some rest. You look tired."

I smile awkwardly, remembering that I haven't seen a mirror since yesterday, and give my fingers a quick run through my hair before he turns and heads for his truck. I turn back to Asher's big, gratitude-filled, blue eyes and wonder what to say next when the sound of his front door opening and slamming shut breaks the silence.

"Daddy!" Hazel cries out, sprinting across the yard toward him.

An attractive brunette woman, the same one I saw drop Hazel off after our riding lesson, follows her out of the house.

"There you are! Henry said he's been looking all over for you two. I thought he was about to call in the National Guard. Glad you're safe. Sorry, I didn't feed her any breakfast yet, but there's been a family emergency, so I have to drop her off a little early."

"Don't sweat it. Thanks for taking her last night, and I hope everything is okay—with the family and all."

"Oh, you never know with that rowdy bunch. I'll call and check in with you later. Bye, sweet girl!" Sam waves goodbye to Asher and Hazel before starting her SUV and flying down the drive before the dust from Dad's truck tires has time to settle.

Asher watches her disappear into the cloud of red dirt, then bends to lift Hazel, giving her a playful spin before propping her on his waist.

"Where were you, daddy?"

"You remember that old apple orchard we like to go to sometimes? Well, I went out there yesterday to show Miss Gemma and the storm trapped us in a barn!"

"A *barn?*" Hazel whispers. "Were you scared?"

Asher chuckles and shakes his head. "No, I wasn't because I wasn't alone. This is Gemma. She's Mr. Carter's daughter."

Hazel smiles, and her eyes light up. The same piercing blue eyes I was looking deep into last night. "Mr. Carter says you live in New York City."

I smile politely back at her and bet she might be the happiest little girl in Sugar Plum. It makes me wonder where her mom is and what happened between her and Asher. Not that it's my place to ask. I don't need to be getting into his business. "That's right. I got hurt really bad, and now there's all kinds of things I don't remember. So, I moved back home to get better."

"What kind of things? Do you know when your birthday is?"

I can't help but laugh at the innocence in her voice. "My dad says it's June 11th. When's your birthday, Hazel?"

"June 23rd."

"Wow! June babies," I say, giving her a high-five. My eyes shift briefly to Asher's, and there's a look in his eyes that makes my heart skip a beat. I wonder what *that's* all about.

"She treats the whole month like it's her birthday." Asher squeezes Hazel's arm playfully, coaxing a high-pitched squeal. "And, just like her dad, she always wants to spend her birthday outside. Doesn't care *how* hot it is."

"Daddy said he'll take me to the big park so we can hike," Hazel says with a twinkle in her eyes.

"Park? I didn't know Sugar Plum had any big parks."

"Big Bend State Park. I want to take her camping so she can see the Milky Way at night," Asher replies. "We haven't taken a trip in forever, so I wanted to do something special this year."

Good dads are so attractive—*especially the tall, dark, and cowboying kind*. Ugh, but no more Gemma. That's the only mushy thought you're allowed to have about Asher for the rest of the day.

"Sounds like fun," I say, returning my attention to Hazel. "I should go take a shower after sleeping on the floor of a barn. We don't want some poor chipmunk to think I'm open for business and come set up shop in my hair, do we? It was nice to meet you, Hazel," I say with a wink and reach out my hand.

Hazel giggles and sticks her hand out to shake mine. "See you later, Alligator!"

"In a while, Crocodile."

I head back to the house, pitching one more look over my shoulder to see Asher lift Hazel onto Scout's saddle. I don't know if kids were ever something I wanted with my big city life or even if I was dating anyone, but the thought of having a family of my own to make memories with someday doesn't sound half bad.

I guess I shouldn't be so doom and gloom about my current situation all the time. It doesn't sound like the version of me that people remember, anyway.

Still, I can't help but wonder how the old version of me would react to someone like Asher. Would I be just as annoyed by him? Intrigued? *Attracted?*

My feelings for him are split three ways, and I don't see things getting any less complicated in the near future. Okay. So maybe I don't have a game plan, but all I know is I better get one fast.

Before I start getting attached to his daughter, too.

# Chapter Eight

**Asher**

Sweat drips down my back as I haul bales of hay into the stable and store them to the side for later use. Dusting off my work gloves, I head out into the blazing sun and roll my neck a few times to loosen the residual tension from sleeping on the floor two nights ago. After our overnight mishap, I've been running behind schedule on all my chores.

Fortunately, there won't be any riding lessons today. Henry says he wants Gemma to get a little more rest, which I agree with. There's no need to push too hard this early in the game, especially when she's already overwhelmed. A little time off won't hurt our progress. Plus, it gives me extra alone time to think.

I shouldn't even think about the boss's daughter, but seeing Gemma interact with Hazel made me feel something. At first, I didn't believe him, but now I think Joshua was right. Maybe the prissy city girl does have a layer of sweet beneath all that sour. It's buried deep, but it's there, alright.

I don't know much about who she used to be, but the person I know her as now might be one of the most intriguing people I've ever met. Sure, she's got that city snark, but she's no pushover. I respect that. She's not afraid to put me in my place, either. Lord knows sometimes I need it.

"Asher!"

I shake the thought when I see Henry heading my way. My blood runs cold in an instant. Oh, boy. What'd I step in this time? "Sir?"

Henry stops a few feet from my front porch and I push out of my chair to greet him. There's something about the way he looks over his shoulder like he's about to deliver news he doesn't want anyone to hear but me. "I'd like to talk to you."

Did he change his mind about me after what happened with Gemma? If he fires me, I'm out of a home, that's for sure. And where would I go? Back to Nashville? Or would I just sulk around Sugar Plum like a kicked dog with his pup, hoping there's room at Motel 6? "Yes, Sir. What about?"

"It's about Gemma." A knot forms in my stomach. "I wanted to let you know that I appreciate you looking after her the other night. Getting her to safety during the storm and all that. Can we, uh— sit?"

"Yes, Sir. Grab a seat. I offer an old, weathered porch chair and lower myself into the other, the knot easing its stronghold as he continues.

"You know, after I lost Camille, I was a wreck. The only thing that kept me together was taking care of Gemma."

I nod in understanding. Hazel's mom didn't die, but she did leave, and stepping up for my daughter was the only thing that got me through the heartache of being tossed aside by the woman I love.

"I was worried when Gemma didn't come home the other night. And for a moment, it was like I was losing her all over again. Now, I'm willing to do everything I can to help her through this difficult time in her life, but I feel like I need to go ahead and tell you that I don't think the two of you should get too close to one another."

"Too close, Sir?" I ask.

Henry gives me a stern look. "Look, Gemma is confused right now. She's trying to navigate this new life while trying to remember her old one. I know she can be a handful, but I saw the way she stuck up for you, and as a father, it concerns me. She's lost. And she just went through a lot of trauma that makes her vulnerable. You're a professional, Asher. That's why I hired you. And I need to know that your intentions with her stay that way."

I'm not sure what I expected from our conversation, but it certainly wasn't the *'no dating my daughter'* talk. "I can assure you nothing is going on between me and Gemma, Sir. Our relationship is strictly professional. I'm just trying to help." I'm shocked he would even think such a thing. In case he hasn't noticed, we aren't exactly pals. I bet his daughter would rather muck out the stable than spend leisure time with me.

Henry searches my eyes. "You're a good man, Asher. I know I can count on you. Just… look after her for me. And if any other cowboys come sniffing around my daughter, feel free to give them my number. I'll set them straight."

"Yes, Sir. I'll do that."

Henry gives a satisfied nod, then returns back to the main house, leaving me alone with my thoughts. Thoughts about the fiery, attractive, and now off-limits girl next door.

Mr. Carter is right. It wouldn't be professional to blur the lines with Gemma, and the last thing I want to do is cross him after all he's done for me. I owe it to him to keep Gemma's best interest in mind. Which means not dating her.

It's a thought that never crossed my mind—until now.

\*\*\*

"Bye, Dad!"

I wave as Hazel sticks an arm out of the open window of her friend's mom's car. I'm wary about letting Hazel go off somewhere without me or Samantha to keep an eye on her, but Hazel and Evie have been friends since kindergarten. It wouldn't hurt to relax and let her have some fun.

I remind myself she's in good hands, then turn, pausing when I see Gemma sitting by herself on the front porch in a bright yellow sundress and a fresh pair of brown leather cowboy boots. With the sun about to set, I'd figure she'd be eating dinner or watching television with her dad, but his truck isn't parked in front of the house.

I rub the back of my neck, my eyes darting between her house and mine. I should probably go home and mind my business, but it's Saturday, and I'm not used to Hazel being gone on a night I don't have to be up early the following day.

Besides, it'd be rude if I didn't at least say hello, seeing as how she's all alone.

She's deep in thought and staring out West when she hears my boots coming up the porch steps. At first, she's slouched, but when she looks over and sees me, she straightens up on the porch swing and casually smooths a hand over her untamed locks of hair. She looks different. More relaxed.

"Partying it up on the porch, huh? I heard you New Yorkers did it up big."

"Sorry, I'll turn it down a notch. Wouldn't want any nosy neighbors to file a noise complaint." Her words are what I'd expect to hear, but their landing is softer and less abrasive than usual.

I laugh, trying to hide any signs of awkwardness, and shrug. "Saw you sitting by yourself and didn't see your dad's truck. Thought I'd come check on you."

"He's out for the night. He went a few towns over for his monthly poker game. Said he'd be back in the morning."

"He left you here alone?" I know Gemma's a grown woman, but it surprises me he'd leave without telling me after our talk. Or... maybe he didn't tell me *because* of our talk?

"Trust me, he didn't want to, but I insisted. I need some time for myself."

"Time to overthink?"

"No," Gemma's face remains soft as she looks back into the horizon. "Just time... to enjoy this beautiful sunset. Besides, not much else to do in this one-horse town, is there?"

An idea pops into my head, though probably not a good one if Mr. Carter had a say about it. But seeing as how he's not here, "Come on. I'm taking you out."

Gemma's expression turns from calm to confused. "What? Out where?" She bites her lip in protest, but I don't take no for an answer.

"It's a surprise. I hope you're hungry," I say, pulling her up from the swing by the hand and leading her down to my truck. One night on the town shouldn't hurt, and it's professional opinion that getting her out might spark an old memory. I mean, it's not like sitting around the house all day has done her a lick of good other than making her a recluse.

I open the passenger door, and Gemma pauses before climbing in. "Another surprise, huh?"

"What? You didn't like the last one?"

"The jury's still out on that one. But I *could* eat."

The houses that pass us by grow in number as we cross through town. Each time we pass a business, she tries to guess where I'm taking her, but I know we're going somewhere she's never been, even if she could remember.

Once we're about ten miles east of town, I turn into the High Moon Saloon parking lot. It doesn't look like much from the outside, but after its grand opening a few years back, it's been dubbed the best honky-tonk west of Lubbock. Since then, people come from all over for live music, dinner, and dancing. The place is packed as usual, and we're lucky to find a spot in the grass behind the gravel lot.

"Surprise, surprise. A country bar. I guess this is where everyone spends their Saturday night, seeing as how it's the only thing in the county open past eight." Gemma unbuckles her seatbelt and climbs out of the cab before I have a chance to get her door. Fortunately, my legs are longer, so I reach the main entrance before she does.

"You shouldn't be so quick with those assumptions. You never know. You just might like it." I flash a winning smile as I hold the door open for her, and she rolls her eyes.

Upbeat country music pours into the parking lot, and Gemma's jaw drops as we venture deeper into the bar. A spinning disco ball hangs from the high ceiling, throwing specks of neon light across a crowded dance floor. "Well, what do you think so far?" I shout over the music.

Gemma surveys the room with curious eyes. Just past the main entrance and to the left is a large, horseshoe-shaped bar with a swinging door that leads into the kitchen. On either side of the dance floor are two long rails with tops wide enough for people to pull up a bar stool, sit, and rest their drinks as they watch and listen. Behind each rail, along the walls, are rows of round bar tables lit by candles, where patrons can sit and dine. And the far end, just past the dance floor, is a large stage with a five-piece band running through a set.

"Is that... line dancing?!"

"Sure is! Why don't you grab that table over there, and I'll get us a couple of drinks!" I point to one of the empty tables next to the dance floor, and she nods.

"Nothing that tastes like pee!" she shouts.

"You remember what pee tastes like?! That's progress!" She gives my shoulder a shove, and I chuckle, my eyes following her until she's perched safely in her chair. I walk over to the bar and order two glasses of water, a Shiner Bock, and something light and fruity to ease her into the new atmosphere. After I pay, I turn and see some guy in a black cowboy hat trying to drag her onto the dance floor.

Picking up on her nervous laughter, I head over and place our drinks on the table before tapping on the guy's shoulder. "Mind if I steal her back, brother?"

The guy whips around, and I brace myself for a fist flying in the direction of my face. There's no telling how I'm gonna get out of this one when Mr. Carter finds out.

Only, there's no fist. It's obvious he's had a few too many since he's been here, but his angry scowl fades to a goofy grin the minute he sees my face. "Holy cow, you're Asher Davidson!"

"Excuse me?" I almost choke on the words as they leave my mouth.

"I saw you last year at the Austin Rodeo. You almost took first place in the bull riding! You're a legend, man!"

"Hey, thanks a lot, man. But, uh... do you mind?"

"Oh! Sorry about that, Ash. I didn't know she was your girl." He drops Gemma's hand and steps back, tipping his hat before disappearing into the crowd.

I turn to Gemma, who stares with wide eyes and a smile as wide as the Rio Grande. "I see how it is. I turn my back for one second, and already you find yourself another dance partner."

Gemma's smile turns bashful as she tears her eyes away from mine, redirecting her gaze to the rhythmic stomps and shimmies out on the floor. "Oh, no. I'm pretty sure I have no idea how to dance like that!"

I click my tongue at her as I take her hand, slowly leading us back into the line of people. "Well then, I guess it's time you learn. Follow my lead, sweetheart."

"Asher!"

With a grin, I tug her along as the band plays a crowd favorite, "Boot Scootin' Boogie." First, we grapevine to the right, then to the left. She stumbles with the heel switches and toe taps but picks it right back up with the toe struts, ending with the Charleston, as we turn to start back at the top. "Move those hips, girl. Loosen up."

Gemma cracks a smile as she mirrors my feet, and before we know it, our hips are swaying in unison. She might not remember dancing, but there's no way this is her first time.

"I think I'm getting it!"

"You sure are," I say, realizing for the first time that our fingers are twined together. Holding her hands while we dance feels so natural that I don't want to break it.

When the song ends, Gemma glances up and hits me with a look that feels like a punch to the chest. I don't think I've ever seen her this happy before. Maybe it's just my ego, but I can't help feeling a swell of pride knowing I did that for her.

It's as unexpected as it is gratifying.

When the first note of the next song rings out, I playfully twirl her toward me, placing one hand firmly on the small of her back and holding the other out to the side as I lead her in a two-step around the dance floor.

*I remember when I met you.*

*I was a big-city boy with small-town blues.*

*This place seemed so small to me.*

Gemma's eyes look deep into mine as I press a hip deep into her, steadying us both as we sway.

*Well, I was used to the Boulevard*
*But when I saw you, I fell so hard.*
*Now, I never wanna leave.*

Gemma pulls her hand from my shoulder, placing it on my chest as she rests her cheek over it, her feet never missing a step. She must remember this, too.

*Girl, I'm here forever.*
*We got moonlight.*
*All night.*
*Lord, I pray on the next star I see tonight,*
*We never lose this thing we've found.*

Having her so close and smelling the scent of sweet apples from her shampoo is enough to break apart my resolve. I let go of her hand and tilt her chin up ever so slightly, then lean in, pressing my lips against hers in a soft kiss. My heart stops the moment our lips touch.

Gemma resists at first, then relaxes and gently wraps her arms around my neck as I lean deeper into the kiss.

*You by my side.*
*I can do without the city lights.*
*I fly so high when you're around,*
*That my feet don't touch the ground.*

I swear there's a current running through us that crackles and sparks each second our lips are locked. It's a feeling so intense that I wouldn't be surprised if the overhead lights started to explode, sending down sparks of electricity like rain. I might deny it if anyone ever asked, but tonight, on the dance floor, Gemma Carter is the first woman ever to send a shiver down my spine.

When this song ends, I step away, and she does the same. Her eyes are wide with a look of something I can't quite make out. Fear? Regret? *Guilt?*

I don't know where her sense of guilt would be coming from, but I know where mine does. Kissing Gemma after her father laid down the law feels like the ultimate betrayal. He trusted me, and I let him down.

"It's getting late. I should probably get you back home."

Gemma doesn't say another word the entire drive home. Heck, she doesn't even bother looking at me. Not that it matters. I can't bring myself to look at her either.

We both know we messed up, but I can't help but wonder how tonight would play out if things were different. What if I wasn't just another distraction on her road to recovery? And what if her dad wasn't my boss? Would I still hate myself as much as I do?

I don't know the answer to those questions, but as I pull up to her house and watch her rush inside without so much as a wave, there's one thing I know for sure. Gemma's not just another city girl to me. Or someone I'm giving horseback riding lessons to. Or my boss' daughter. Not anymore.

And deep down, I know that pursuing any relationship with her that's more than platonic spells trouble. Pure, hard to resist T-R-O-U-B-L-E.

# Chapter Nine

**Gemma**

It's the day after my dance floor escapades with Asher at the High Moon Saloon, and I decide it might be best to get away for a while. Luckily, Dad agrees to drop me off in town before running his morning errands. He's leery at first. I know he doesn't like the idea of me wandering around the square all alone. But after sitting him down to discuss healthy boundaries moving forward, he gives up without further argument.

I spend most of the morning strolling up and down sidewalks, window shopping, until I see something I can't live without, then stop dead in my tracks when I see a local street vendor selling fresh apples. Just as I'm on the verge of asking the man behind the counter where they're from, a young couple passes by, laughing and holding hands as they lean into one another. My chest aches as my mind drifts back to last night and my earth-shattering lip lock with Asher.

I feel like a teenager who just had her first kiss. Because technically, it *was* my first kiss. At least, for all I know. I wouldn't remember any of my past kissing partners, if there were any, of course. But if I were a betting woman, I'd say his kiss takes the cake. The way he rescued me from that cowboy, then held me close, knowing exactly how to lead me around that hardwood floor. It's like I was dancing on air. Like I really was his girl.

But all good things must come to an end, right? I can't expect to two-step my way into his life when my own is such a trainwreck. It wouldn't be fair. All the warm, fuzzy feelings about him and the kiss we shared are just fantasies of a relationship never meant to be. Besides, I saw the look in his eyes when he pulled away. I might not remember last week, but I wasn't born yesterday, and I know regret when I see it.

My face burns with embarrassment as I drop my eyes, wishing I could disappear into thin air until a quiet voice reminds me, "Never let them see you cry."

Before the apple vendor has time to notice me, I duck my head and push through the door of the nearest boutique, greeted by a familiar chime from the bell above the doorway.

"Gemma? Oh my gosh!" Olivia's eyes light up from behind the counter, and I can feel the blood as it drains from my face. "I was wondering when I'd see you again. Give me just a minute to figure this out, and I'll be right with you."

My tension eases when her eyes drop to the polka-dot blouse on the counter, grateful to catch her when she's busy. Because today is not a good day for me to be the center of *anyone's* attention. I take a few cautious steps in her direction, my curiosity rising as I watch her fish a needle with white thread through the delicate fabric. It looks like she's trying to fix a small tear in the sleeve, but her stitch is awkward and misplaced.

She groans and shakes her head. "Ugh, I don't know why I can't get this."

I stop on the other side of the counter and lean in for a closer look. "I think you're positioning your hands wrong."

Olivia raises a brow. "Do you know how to hand stitch? Oh my gosh, I'd love some help. I've been at it for over half an hour now."

I reach out and take the needle from her, using my other hand to bring the sleeve in close. I don't know what causes me to think I know what I'm doing, but my fingers work precisely as I push the needle through the fabric and finish mending the hole.

After I secure my stitch, Olivia cuts away the loose ends with a tiny pair of sewing scissors and holds the blouse up to inspect it.

"Just… Wow!" She neatly folds the blouse and sets it down on the counter. "Gemma, that was amazing. You *know* you went to fashion school in New York, right? You had to have remembered how to do that."

"Fashion school," I repeat the words as though saying them out loud will be enough to spark something new. But nothing comes to mind. The only memory I have is from after the crash when Dad told me I worked in the fashion industry in New York.

"It's okay. You at least have to let me buy you a cup of coffee, though. I'd still be here poking a hundred holes in that shirt if it wasn't for you."

"Now, you're speaking my language. I don't think I've had a decent cup of coffee since I've been here." A wave of relief washes over me when she doesn't press the issue with fashion school. Maybe making a few close friends I can trust will be easier than I thought. Anything's gotta be better than being stuck back home with my dad and Asher all day.

Olivia grabs her purse from under the counter and fishes out an obscenely large set of keys, then flips over the sign on the door to read CLOSED and locks up behind us on our way out. It's half past noon when we cross the street to a small coffee shop called Sugar and Cream.

The place is buzzing with high school students on their lunch break, but fortunately, we're able to find a small empty table by the front window after the barista whips up two vanilla lattes with extra shots of espresso.

"So, how are the riding lessons coming along?"

"They're not bad. I still need more practice getting on and off, but I like the riding part, and Asher is.... He's okay."

"*Just* okay?" Olivia sits across from me with an eager look on her face. Almost *too* eager.

"Well, if we're being completely honest, he can be a real jerk sometimes." I'm not sure who my words shock more—Olivia or myself.

"He sure is something, isn't he?" Olivia laughs. "I know he likes to get a rise out of people, but once you get to know him, he's one of the most humble, hardworking people you'll ever meet. One thing you always have to remember about Asher—If he doesn't like you, he's just not gonna talk to you."

"Oh, is *that* what it is?" I laugh and take another sip, secretly hoping Asher doesn't really hate my guts after all. "So... how long has it been just him and Hazel?"

Olivia hums, tapping her long, natural nails on the table. "I think a few years now. That's when he moved to Sugar Plum and started working for your dad, at least. I've never heard him talk about Hazel's mom, but Joshua says that whatever happened hurt him a lot."

Thinking about Asher getting his heart broken throws me for a loop. I guess I always assumed he'd have been the one to break someone's heart. I frown, wondering if Hazel remembers what happened. "That's terrible. That could explain why he's so short-tempered with me, but you'd never guess it by the way he is with his daughter."

"Oh, yeah. Asher's a great dad. If we're being honest, he's the talk of the town in all the major sewing circles, if you know what I mean."

I lift an eyebrow at her. "Like... women who want to date him?"

"You didn't hear it from me, but Joshua teases him constantly. Tells him he could be Sugar Plum's official bachelor if he wanted to. Asher never was one to date around, though. He's always been too focused on his job, his daughter, and whenever the next rodeo is coming to town."

Is it wrong that I feel a huge relief knowing that Asher doesn't date? I know I have no claim over him, but I'm having a hard enough time coming to terms with that kiss. I'm not sure I could handle knowing I was just another notch on his belt. "Yeah, so tell me more about that. He told me he rides bulls. Is he as good as everyone puffs him up to be?"

"He's no Lane Frost, but he holds his own, I'd say. The man's probably got more belt buckles than the West has tumbleweeds. You should have him show you sometime." The way she smiles and winks suggestively makes me roll my eyes and feel at ease, all at the same time. Something about her makes me feel like we've known each other forever. Although, technically, we have. She's just the only one who remembers it.

"Alright, so I know he gives you a hard time. But how are you two *really* getting along?" She still sounds too curious for this to be a casual question, but I'm not ready to tell her about our romantic stroll through the apple orchard. Or how we slept together in a barn. *Or* about last night when I made a complete fool out of myself and let him give me my first kiss, so to speak. "There's not much to say. As far as I'm concerned, he's all business, and I'm just the boss's daughter."

"Well, you should get to know him better. He can be a really sweet guy if you give him a chance, and I think you two could be a good pair."

My cheeks flush pink, and I look away, hoping she doesn't pick up on the panic in my eyes. Oh, he had his chance, alright. "Oh, I'm not like… trying to date anyone or anything," I say, stumbling over my words more than I mean to.

Olivia laughs and pitches a confused look. "Yeah, I just mean as friends. It would be *crazy* if you two tried to date with everything you've got going on right now."

I'm vying for my own downfall at this point. With a stiff smile, I nod and take a gulp so big it burns on the way down. I wish I didn't let Asher get under my skin like this. Feeling my sense of control unravel while staying determined to get my memories back is exhausting.

"Thanks for the latte. And for the company," I tell Olivia as we cross the street to head back to her shop.

"My pleasure! We should hang out more." The cheerful look on her face remains but doesn't hide the longing I see in her eyes. I wish I could remember how things used to be for us.

Asher insists it's good for me to get out more by myself, which is probably good advice. Not that I'll admit it to him anytime soon, but seeing how it brought me closer to an old friend, I find it one piece of advice I can follow. "That'd be nice. My dad hasn't taken me to get a new phone yet, but I'm sure you know how to get ahold of me better than I do."

Olivia laughs as we reach the door to her boutique. "I'll have my guy call your guy?"

Thinking about Asher as 'my guy' is enough to make my skin crawl. Like I need another reason to talk to him outside our lessons. "Sounds good."

"So, what are you doing the rest of the afternoon? Are you busy? We just got a new shipment of clothes this week that I know you're gonna love."

Thinking about all the trouble I could get into with Dad's credit card, I watch in anticipation as she unlocks the door, pushes it open, and the bell chimes.

# Chapter Ten

**Asher**

The wood floor of our tiny two-bedroom home rattles beneath my boots as I haul my gear from my bedroom out to the truck. I was excited when I got the call about a contest in Amarillo. This will be my first event of the year since Austin.

Given everything that happened with Gemma and her returning home, I had to put my rodeo career on the back burner while I helped Mr. Carter. I had no idea how big of a rift she'd cause, but because Amarillo is only a two-and-a-half-hour drive, I don't think Mr. Carter will mind if I take a Friday off.

That, and I think blowing off some steam is a good idea, too.

When I get to my truck, I toss my gear bag into the passenger's seat, pausing when I see movement coming from the Carter's front porch. I shouldn't be surprised to see Gemma rocking in the swing all by herself. It looks like she's reading a magazine or something.

A sudden urge to go talk to her tugs me in her direction, but I push back as hard as I can. We haven't spoken much lately since she started investing her time in other things, and our riding lessons have been postponed for the week. I'm not sure what 'other things' there are, but I don't argue with one less chore on my to-do list.

A part of me wonders if it's a cover for her not wanting to see my sorry face. I can't say I'd blame her if that were the case. That kiss we shared was electric, but it sent a shock through the already complicated dynamic of our relationship. A shock that neither of us are willing to admit to. Life would be so much easier if I could hit the rewind button and go back to the way things were before I screwed them up. Because even when we're at each other's throats, at least we'd be talking to each other.

When I make it back inside, I feel my phone vibrate in my back pocket. I pull it and check the screen. It's Sam. She's supposed to be on her way over to watch Hazel while I'm out of town. She must be running behind.

"Hey there, Sam. Everything alright?"

"I'm afraid not. I was packing a bag to head over when I got the call. My uncle's been real sick, and they've got him in a hospital in Lubbock. They're saying he took a turn for the worse this morning, and now Paw wants me to drive him out there to see him."

"I'm sorry to hear that. Yeah, you should definitely get your paw to Lubbock. And be safe now. You can keep me posted when you get there, and I'll figure out what to do with Hazel in the meantime." I glance down at my watch. Only thirty minutes before I have to head out if I'm going to make it on time.

"You sure? I hate leaving you like this when I know you're trying to leave town, yourself."

"Don't worry about me. Family comes first, you know that."

"You're one of a kind, Ash. Thanks for understanding. Oh, and tell Hazel we'll finish that rainforest puzzle when I get back to town."

"Will do, Sam. You take care." I disconnect the call, and the sound of Hazel playing in her room has me troubleshooting how I'll find a sitter last minute and still be on the road on time. I rub the back of my neck and walk back to my truck as a possible solution pops into my head.

But it's not one I'm happy about.

I know I'm the last one she wants to see right now, and, for all I know, she could tell me to drop dead. But Henry's truck is gone, and I don't have anyone else to call.

I climb the steps like a dog with his tail between his legs. "Hey there, Gemma."

Gemma closes last month's issue of Texas Monthly and places it in her lap. "Asher."

I'm unsure what I expect, but it certainly isn't the smile she flashes in my direction. At first, I'm stumped on what to say. It's like all the words I know disappear from my mind, leaving me staring like a deer in headlights until I remember what brought me over in the first place.

"I guess there's no easy way to say this, so I'm just gonna come right out and say it." Sweat forms on the palms of my hands. "I need to ask you for a favor. Feel free to say no if you're not comfortable with it, but if you can help, I'd be in your debt."

Gemma frowns. Then, she raises a brow as the corner of her mouth curls up, and her eyes sparkle with wonder. "Oh, really? I can have some fun with that."

I use the back of my pants to dry my sweaty palms and maintain my serious tone. "I have a competition tonight in Amarillo, and Hazel's nanny just called to tell me she's heading out of town for a family emergency."

Her look of wonder quickly turns to panic when she realizes what I'm about to ask.

I hold up a hand, shielding myself from any premature rejection. "Like I said, you don't have to if you're uncomfortable. But there's money on the counter for pizza, the fridge and pantries are stocked, and she is really, *really* looking forward to a girl's night tonight."

"How long are we talking here?"

"Just until I get home. It'll be after midnight, but she should be out before that."

Gemma furrows her brows and stays quiet for a moment. "Does she... have any allergies? And what do I do if there's an emergency? I don't have a phone."

I smile. "No allergies. And there's a landline inside. My cell number is on the fridge. If it gets too much for you, take her to your place until your dad gets home. He'll know what to do from there."

Gemma's eyes flash to my house. "What if she doesn't like me?"

I chuckle and motion for her to follow me. "Only one way to find out."

"Are you just asking because I live next door?" Gemma asks, stumbling down the steps behind me.

"Wouldn't know you to ask if you didn't. But no. It's not *just* because you live next door. I don't leave Hazel with people I don't trust. And I trust you."

"Oh."

"And besides, she talks about you all the time. Sometimes, she won't shut up about you. This will get her off my back about asking so many questions."

"Whatever. You're embellishing."

"I am not. She's been asking questions every day since you've been here. What's your favorite color? Do you know how to swim? What's your favorite kind of rock? Do you like ice cream?"

"Alright, alright. I get it." Gemma's eyes grow soft when we reach my front door, but as I turn the knob to let her inside, I'm hit with a wave of concern.

What if Hazel and Gemma become close? Will that make me want to be closer to her, too? It's hard to forget what happened last time I got too close to Gemma.

"Haze, come out here!" I lead Gemma into the small living room and pause until I hear Hazel's footsteps coming down the hall.

A smile beams across her face when she lays eyes on Gemma. "Gemma! I was waiting for you to visit me."

I flash a victorious grin. "Told you."

Gemma smirks and steps closer to Hazel, crouching down so they're both at eye level. "I've been meaning to. How have you been?"

"Good! I caught a butterfly yesterday," Hazel says, with a look of pride. "Daddy told me to let it go so that it can find its family."

Gemma glances up at me. "That was good advice. Everyone needs family."

Since our move to Texas, Samantha and Mr. Carter have been the closest thing to family we've had. Sure, Hazel still loves going to Nashville every year to see my parents, but it's been hard for her not having her mom in the picture. Sometimes, I feel like she's being cheated out of her childhood and all the memories they could be making together.

"Hazel, Sam had to go see her family out of town tonight, so she can't come stay with you while I'm gone. But if you're okay with it, I was thinking Gemma could watch you instead. What do you think?"

Hazel bounces up and down and cheers. "Yes! Yes! Yes! Can I show her my rock collection?"

I chuckle, scratching my jaw through my beard. "She likes collecting rocks with funny shapes. She's going to ask what you think each one looks like."

Gemma clicks her tongue and gives an approving nod. "Well, I think that sounds fun."

"Hooray! I'll go get my collection," Hazel says before darting out of the room.

I reach out to place a cautious hand on the back of Gemma's arm, then move closer to her so she can hear when I lower my voice. "Are you sure you're okay with watching her? There's still time to back out, you know."

Gemma smirks, and all the feelings of electricity between us come surging back like someone flipped a switch. "What? And miss an opportunity to get all the good dirt on you? Not on your life, Cowboy."

I mirror her smirk for a moment before looking deep into her eyes. "Well, like I said, this means a lot to me."

Gemma's eyes drop and briefly pause on my lips before returning. "It's not a problem, really. Anything to get me out of the house, right?"

I let out a nervous laugh. If she keeps saying all the right things, it'll take every ounce of willpower not to push her against the wall and kiss right here and now.

"I do have one condition, though."

Her words throw me. "What's that?"

Gemma radiates a smile that makes my heart forget how to beat. "Bring home a win."

I give a determined nod and a wink for good measure. "Yes, ma'am."

Gemma studies my eyes for another long moment before Hazel busts in with a clear, plastic box of rocks. "Here they are! Gemma, look!"

"Wow." Gemma's look is priceless as she studies Hazel's treasure chest of weird and ugly rocks. "Now, *that's* a collection."

Hazel tends to catch people off-guard, but it's what I love about her the most. She's a chip off the old block when it comes to shock value.

"Now, before you get into them, come give Dad a hug. It's time for me to go."

Hazel carefully hands the box off to Gemma before crashing into my arms—this time, squeezing extra tight. I notice she gets this way anytime I leave to go ride. "Good luck, Daddy."

"Aww, thanks, Sweetpea. " I plant a kiss on her cheek, then straighten up to grab my hat off the wall. When I turn to Gemma, I notice a tender look in her eyes before I mouth the words, "Thank you."

She waves her hand and shoos me out onto the porch. "Break a leg—er... I mean... good luck!"

I smile and shake my head, giving her a tip of my hat before turning toward my truck. When I make my way down the drive, my eyes wander to the rear-view mirror, where I can see Gemma and Hazel waving from the porch.

My heart stops as the fantasy of having a complete family flashes through my mind. The thought passes as quickly as it comes, but it's still enough to knock the wind out of my lungs.

I've always considered myself a realist. And I certainly don't entertain such frivolous thoughts when it comes to relationships. But I can't deny the burning feeling in my chest when this particular one starts to fade. Family. Wife. Mother. These are all words I buried deep a long time ago until this insufferable woman decided to dig a hole to China by way of my heart.

And now, here they are—brought to the surface for all the world to see. Is it crazy to think about Gemma this way when I know what's all at stake? Yeah. But probably just as crazy as me thinking that I can swallow down the horse pill of growing feelings I have for her without something strong to chase it with.

With one hand gripping the wheel tight, I turn on the radio and flip through the stations until I find some old country song more troubled than me.

And just my luck, this one's about a woman, too.

# Chapter Eleven

**Gemma**

As I watch Asher's truck disappear, anxiety rears its ugly head. I'm alone with his daughter—the most important person in the world to him. What if I screw up? What if she *hates* me?

Every concerning scenario pops into my head as I lead Hazel back inside the house. Surely, I don't know the first thing about caring for a child... or do I? It doesn't seem like it would be all that hard. If it weren't for all the pressure I feel because it's *his* daughter I'm left to care for.

"Okay. You pick a movie to watch, and I'll go get my toys so we can play," Hazel says before running off and ditching me.

Snooping is such a strong word. So, when she's gone, I decide to explore. The living room is what you'd expect. There's a simple brown leather couch with a matching recliner, a hand-made wooden coffee table, and a flat-screen television mounted to the wall with a small media cabinet below. What catches my eye is the rustic bookshelf in the corner, its top half filled with trophies and shiny silver and gold belt buckles.

Many only have images, but some have words inscribed on them, as well. *Men's Bull Riding Division - 1st Place. Sun Bowl Rodeo. El Paso, TX. Bull Rider's Showdown - 2022.*

*Texas Rodeo Circuit Finals Winner.*

*2nd Place - Men's Bull Riding. Austin Rodeo - 2023.*

Wow, he really *is* good. I don't know the ins and outs of bull riding, but from what I've seen on TV, it's a highly competitive and athletic sport. I suppose that's part of the reason why Asher is so... BIG. An uncontrollable smile breaks across my face as I quickly scold myself.

Get a grip, Gemma. He's not a slab of meat.

"I got my toys!" Hazel's sudden shout nearly has me jumping out of my skin.

I whip around with an innocent smile and watch her lay out a few animal figurines, what looks like the pieces of a science kit, and three jars of Play-Doh on the coffee table. Interesting choices for an interesting little girl. "Cool! I still need to pick out a movie, though."

"Oh! I'll pick!" Springing up, she rounds the coffee table and gets on her knees to view the shelves with the DVDs. After rummaging around for a few minutes, she fishes one out of the stack, slides the DVD into the player, and hands me the unfamiliar case. On the cover, there's a large blue animated fish with yellow fins swimming in the ocean. *Finding Dory.*

She takes a spot on the floor beside me and says, matter-of-factly, "You're kinda like Dory. She can't remember things, either."

I'm unsure how to feel about being compared to an absent-minded fish, but I know she means no harm. "Sort of. She can't make new memories, and I can't remember the old ones."

Hazel frowns with curious eyes. "How do you get them back?"

"The doctors don't know. What works for some people is different for others. But sometimes, being around familiar things can help." I lean back against the couch and cross my legs, and when Hazel does the same, my heart melts. There's something so comforting about being near her. Maybe it's the innocence. Or the fact that I know I don't have to feel any pressure around her.

My mind wanders, and I think about Asher, who makes me feel the same when he's not stomping on my last nerve. He may not be as pleasant to be around as Hazel is, but they both only know me as the person I am now and not who I used to be.

"Sometimes, I don't remember things either," Hazel says.

"Oh, yeah? Like what?"

"Daddy said I was born in Nashville, but I don't remember which house we lived in. I only remember grandma and grandpa's."

I remember Dad calling Asher a Nashville cowboy, but I'm curious about what made him move all the way out here. And what ever happened with Hazel's mom. Even if he didn't mind talking about it, it seems like too highly personal of a thing to ask about. Especially after the conversation I had with Olivia.

"Do you like it here?" I ask.

Hazel nods and hands me a jar of red Play-Doh. "There's so many animals! And I have lots of friends at school, too."

I smile at the pure happiness in her voice. She's so carefree and optimistic. I wish I could find a way to be more like that. I should be looking forward to tomorrow instead of getting hung up on the past. But that's easier said than done with memory loss. Did I have a lot of friends in New York? Was I even a good person?

Sometimes, I'm *afraid* to remember.

I hear Dad's funny ranch stories and see his proud smile when I like something he cooks, and it reminds me of how lucky I am to have a place I can call home. Talking to Olivia about clothes and the local gossip, riding horses with Asher and learning more and more about him as he peels back the layers, and letting go of my stress to have fun with Hazel—these are all important parts of the new life I'm building here in Sugar Plum.

The movie plays in the background as Hazel and I discuss every topic under the sun. The coolest animals. Her birthday plans for this year. How brave she thinks her dad is for bull riding.

It isn't long before yawns break through her sentences. She rubs her tired eyes and rests her head against the couch cushion behind us. "I'm tired."

I check the clock on the wall, seeing it's almost nine o'clock. Asher was right when he said she wouldn't last long. "How about you go brush your teeth and find some pajamas?"

Moving noticeably slower than before, Hazel gets up and disappears down the hall.

I gather her toys to return to her room and wonder what Asher is doing now. Maybe he's sitting in the bleachers talking with his buddies or in the middle of a giant arena having the ride of his life. I hope he tells me all about it when he returns.

"Goodnight, Hazel," I say as I tuck her in, patting down her bright pink and purple My Little Pony comforter.

Hazel's eyes are half-lidded as she sinks into the softness of her pillow and hugs a small stuffed elephant against her side. "Are you coming back tomorrow?"

I try to hide a look of panic. Hazel's a great kid, but I warned myself about this. I need to be responsible. Getting too close and not taking care of my own problems before crashing into someone else's life is pretty high on my current list of concerns.

"Maybe not tomorrow. But soon."

Hazel's eyes flutter shut, and she dozes off before she can answer.

I quietly creep out of her bedroom, leaving her door cracked, before plopping down on the couch and falling asleep to a documentary about an octopus. When I hear the rattle of keys unlocking the front door, my heart leaps into my throat, and I'm on my feet in a flash.

The door opens quietly, and Asher stops when he spots me hovering by the couch. A slight grin flashes across his face as he tip-toes in my direction. "Is she asleep?"

I nod. "We had fun. She really wore herself out, though," I whisper.

Asher's eyes light up, and he chuckles softly. "Oh, I'm sure she'll talk my ear off about it tomorrow. Thank you, again, for helping out tonight."

"Are you kidding me? I should be the one thanking you. I get so bored over at the main house. Besides, Hazel's a sweetheart. If you're ever in another jam, I'd gladly volunteer."

Asher raises a brow. "*Really?* Great. I'll keep that in mind."

I doubt he expected me to enjoy being stuck in an unfamiliar place with another stranger. But then again, neither did I. Something tells me he and his daughter have a habit of catching people off guard.

"So... how was it? I saw your collection of belt buckles. I must say, I'm impressed. I bet you did pretty well tonight." I regret my words as soon as they leave my mouth.

*Great.* Now, I probably sound like some star-struck teenager gawking over the star athlete who gave her her first kiss.

Asher glances over at the shelf before flashing me an amused look. "Impressed, huh?"

It could be my eyes playing tricks on me in the dark, but I swear he looks a little smug. *Of course,* he did well.

I know I haven't known him long, but Asher strikes me as the kind of guy who'd sulk for days if he performed poorly. He must be riding high off a good rodeo, or there's no way he'd be so chipper. My logic tells me I should hate him by principle alone, but there's something about the sparkle in his eyes when he challenges me that makes my knees feel like they're made of Jello. It's an uncomfortable sensation, and I wouldn't say I like it one bit.

"As if your ego needs *any* more reassurance," I say, making sure he catches my exaggerated eye roll. "You didn't answer my question. Did you place?"

Asher scoffs. "Excuse me, I happen to be a very humble human being. But since you asked, I placed first." He flashes me a smile so dazzling white that it's a wonder why women aren't lined up outside his door.

I can't say I'm surprised by the news. I've seen him ride a horse and know how stubborn he is. I can only imagine his stubbornness when a bull tries to buck him off its back.

"Did you win a buckle?"

Asher shakes his head. "No. No buckle this time. They don't give them out for the smaller rodeos. Just cash prizes." He pauses and eyes me before the corner of his mouth turns up slightly. "Doesn't matter though. I mean... not to sound all like some country bumpkin, but the best prize you can win around here is respect. Wouldn't expect some big city girl to understand the rules of a small town."

I stifle a laugh. Of course, he's going to find a way to take a dig wherever he can. But our conversations aren't as sharp and aggressive as they used to be. They're more... playful. Flirtatious even. I may not be ready to let him off the hook for all his stormy moods, but at least I'm starting to see the sun break through the clouds more often.

"In case you didn't get the memo, this city girl's roots are planted deep in the heart of Texas."

"Well, look at you, Miss Fancy Pants. You're starting to sound more like one of us by the day."

My feelings are torn when the truth of our conversation starts to hit a little too close to home. A part of me is happy because I fit in more without having to remember my past here, but if my life is back in New York, maybe I should feel the opposite.

Surely, there was a reason the old me left in the first place. And if those memories return, would I still feel the same way about Texas? Or Sugar Plum? I shake the thoughts before I say something I'll regret. "Well, I'm glad everything went well for you tonight. I don't know much about rodeos, but they sound exciting."

Asher's eyes light up. "You should come with me to my next competition. "

My eyes grow wide. "What? Really?"

Asher shrugs. "Why not? It's just up the road in Lubbock. If your dad's alright with it, it might be good for you to get out of town and have some fun."

I cross my arms over my chest, shooting him a smirk and remembering what happened the *last* time he took me out for a night of fun. "Like you need another cheerleader in the stands," I say dryly.

"You'd cheer for me, too? Well, ain't that sweet?"

I know my face must be lighting up every possible shade of pink by the stupid smile on Asher's face. He holds my gaze until I give in and crack a smile. "Thanks for the invite. I'll talk to my dad and see what he thinks."

"I think you'd like it. Plenty of good people watching to be had. Plus, it'd be nice to have someone to talk to. Those drives sure do get lonely." When Asher takes a step back, my body feels colder. I'm not sure if I'm the best person to keep him company late at night when his loneliness starts to kick in, but the rodeo idea sounds fantastic.

My mind adds the number of times he must have traveled by himself, and I can't help the ache in my chest when I think about him competing without anyone he knows in the stands. He seems to love the sport enough not to mind, but it makes me hope even more that Dad lets me go. And if he plays his cards right, I may even cheer for him.

I look at the clock on the wall, and it's almost one in the morning. "I... I should probably head back. It's late."

Asher nods and walks me onto the porch, pausing as he watches me cross the field to the main house. I'm still close enough to hear him say, "Goodnight, Gemma."

While watching Asher ride sounds exhilarating, it's equally as terrifying to think about how badly he could get hurt. But that doesn't stop the sudden longing for a big, strong man in cowboy boots to sweep me off my feet, strap me onto the back of his horse, and ride me off into the sunset.

I scold myself for having such thoughts, but not before wondering if I was the same species of hopeless romantic in my past life.

"See you bright and early," I say, not missing the glimmer of hope I see in Asher's eyes when I turn to wave goodnight. When I pass the riding stables, I try to think of other things I can do to help uncover my past, but it's a lost cause.

It's hard trying to think about the past when all I can think about is the future—the future—and Asher... in a tight pair of Wrangler jeans.

# Chapter Twelve

**Asher**

I'm midway through my morning chores when I hear a sudden scream. Hazel's scream.

"Dad!"

I lift my head from tending to Ginger, one of the ranch's dairy cows. When I hear it for the second time, my body goes into fight or flight, and I nearly knock over the pail of milk I spent twenty minutes filling.

"Dad!"

I run out of the barn, my eyes darting around until I spot Hazel standing by the wooden chicken coop. She has the roof of the nesting box propped open as she balances on her toes to look inside.

When I reach her, I place a hand on her shoulder and look her over, making sure she wasn't pecked or something. Doubtful given the kind nature of our chickens, but still.

"Are you okay? What's wrong?"

"Daisy's eggs hatched!" Hazel turns to face me with an excited look on her face.

Relief washes over me, and I lean to investigate. Sure enough, there they are—four fluffy chicks in Daisy's nest. "Well, it's about time. They must've hatched overnight."

Hazel perches her hands on the edge of the nesting box to watch Daisy walk around inside the coop, her chicks following her. "We have to name them!"

It'll be hard to tell them apart, with them all being yellow, but I smile and nod. "Alright, what should we call that one?"

Hazel follows my finger as I point to the one staying closest to its mom's side.

"Nugget."

I stifle a laugh. I don't think she realizes it, but the last thing I want to do is rain on her baby chicken parade. We both agree on Minnie, Honey, and Comet for the other three and huddle close as we watch the tiny chicks swarm their mom.

"She's a good mom. I wish I had a mom like her."

A frown settles when I look over just in time to see her face fall. It's never easy talking about her mom, especially when she has so many questions about her or why she left. Unfortunately, I don't have all the answers for her, but the ones I do have aren't pretty.

"I know, Sweetpea. You and I are a team, though, remember?" I tell her the same thing I always say when she gets like this, mainly for a lack of anything better to say.

"I know," she says, wrapping her arms around my neck and sighing. "I just want a mom. A real mom."

Hazel's right. She deserves a mother who actually cares about her. Not one who leaves when she's only three years old to start a new family with another man. I can handle her not wanting a life with me when I was on the road all the time, but how could a woman leave her only child to go have another with the next guy?

Pain grips my chest like a vice, and I feel it shake throughout my entire body. It's one thing for Hazel's mom to make me feel like I wasn't good enough to keep her around, but she made our daughter feel like she wasn't good enough, either. It's enough to make me never want to trust a woman again.

I still wish she had a mom, though. Finding a good woman for Hazel to look up to would be nice, but it would take someone extraordinary to fill those shoes.

Someone I trust. Someone who Hazel loves being around. Someone who… clicks.

It's no surprise when Gemma crosses my mind, knowing how she hits so many of those marks. But life isn't as simple as checking things off a list. Things are complicated, and Gemma has her own life to figure out. That'd be a lot of pressure to put on her, even if I was ready to entertain the idea.

Not to mention how Mr. Carter would feel after making it *crystal clear* that he doesn't approve of anyone, including me, dating his daughter in the condition she's in. Do I really want to cross the man responsible for helping me get back on my feet when it comes to the most important person in his life?

Talk about playing with fire.

Luckily, Hazel gets distracted by the chicks again, and the tense moment rolls past us like a cloud. The sun breaks free again, and I'm just grateful that most moments are sunny for her. The world around her can get pretty dark, and if I can protect her from that for as long as I can, I will.

That means being mindful of my decisions and the consequences that may result in the aftermath.

After so much excitement and a bath to wash off all the mud she jumped around in earlier this morning, Hazel takes a nap just in time for riding lessons. I sneak out of the house and find Gemma waiting for me in the stable. There's really nothing left to teach her at this point, and I'm pretty sure if any of this was supposed to jog her memory that it would've by now.

But I've been wrong before.

"Moving slow today," Gemma says with a cute smirk. The way she gracefully climbs onto Sunshine's back makes her look like she's been practicing in her sleep.

I chuckle and put on Scout's gear as she leads Sunshine out of the stable. She's been wearing new clothes lately that I can only guess Olivia helped her pick out. A nice pair of boot-cut jeans and an off-white t-shirt with brown cowboy boots are enough to get a cowboy's heart racing.

Not that she looked terrible in the clothes she brought from New York, but they made her stick out like a sore thumb. Seeing her in something like this, though... let's say it better suits her personality. Like these are the kind of clothes she's meant to be wearing. And the way she looks so comfortable right now with her right hand perfectly gripping the reins and her smile glowing. A woman like that belongs in the country.

She turns expectantly, and all I can do is stare.

"What? Is my form off?" Gemma straightens out her back and relaxes her shoulders.

I shake my head as I tear my eyes away. "Nope, posture's fine. Go on ahead. I'll catch up."

Gemma's eyes linger on mine momentarily, and I expect a protest. But instead, she merely nods and coaxes Sunshine outside.

I finish tightening Scout's saddle before mounting him, then nudge his sides with my heels to go. When I see Gemma riding ahead, I dig my heels deeper into Scout's sides and grip the reins. I blow right past Gemma, "Moving slow today!"

Gemma laughs and narrows her eyes with determination before gripping Sunshine's reins and prompting the start of a friendly race between the two of us.

We ride quickly through the large field of grass that stretches back toward the tree line where the orchard lies. The wind flies through my hair, tugging at the long sleeves of my shirt while the sound of Scout's hooves thunder beneath me. It's like I'm flying only a few feet above the ground.

Before we reach the orchard, we slow down to a more steady pace, riding alongside each other as our nearly breathless laughter dies. Gemma's eyes sparkle as she places her right hand over her heart. "What a rush!"

"You're welcome to come out here anytime, you know. You've got it down enough to come out here by yourself. Pretty sure your dad wouldn't mind either."

Gemma nods and gives a bashful smile. "Yeah, maybe. I've just been staying busy in the house lately."

"You still looking through all those photo albums? They're bound to help if you keep at it."

"I've looked at every picture a hundred times and still don't remember anything. But I did find an old empty sketchbook in my room. It's been good making time to sit down and draw. I've even been trying my hand at clothing design."

"Clothing design, eh?" I think about Hazel's excitement whenever I bring home a new coloring book and a box of crayons, then try to imagine Gemma sprawled out on her bed with her pencils and charcoal or whatever she uses to sketch.

"Dad even dug my mom's old sewing machine out of storage and wants to take me to the fabric store in town to see if I still know how to use it. He said she taught me how to sew when I was still in elementary school."

"Well, look at you. Sugar Plum's next top fashion designer."

Gemma gives a wry smile and rolls her eyes. "Hey, no promises I'll be any good at it. I just know it's something that feels... right. It makes me happy."

"That's all that matters, isn't it?"

"Yeah, I guess so. I mean, that and getting my memories back."

"What will you do if you get them back? Go back to the city?" I know it's a stupid question as soon as the words leave my mouth.

Gemma's eyes widen in surprise. "Oh... I don't know. I haven't really thought—"

Before she finishes her sentence, a rattlesnake slithers across a large rock less than five feet ahead and sends the horses into a frenzy. Sunshine rears, knocking Gemma off balance and sending her down into a patch of mud as the snake disappears into the tall grass.

My heart feels like it might beat out of my chest, and within seconds, I'm on the ground and by her side. She slowly sits up, her new shirt and jeans rocking the latest in mud couture. I crouch in front of her and reach out for her to take my hand when I see the shock in her eyes.

"Gemma, hey." I snap my fingers in front of her face. "You okay? Did you hit your head? Are you hurt?"

Silence.

"Gemma?" *Please, Lord, don't let her have a concussion!*

The alarmed look on her face fades, replaced by one of insanity, as she starts laughing uncontrollably. Her eyes screw shut as she places a hand on her stomach. "What in the world happened? One moment, I'm on Sunshine. The next, I'm taking a bath in a puddle of mud!"

I crack a relieved smile when I realize that she's okay, but the thought of her getting hurt on my watch does a number on me. "I think she saw a snake or something and got spooked. You sure you're okay?"

Gemma nods, her body still shaking from laughter. "I'm fine. Can't say the same about my clothes, though."

"You know, city girls pay good money for those fancy spa mud baths," I say, pulling her to her feet.

Gemma slips in her mud-caked boots and nearly crashes into my chest. She wraps her fingers around my biceps for balance, then looks up with a flushed look. "Whoa."

I grab her waist to steady her, privy to the fact that the mud she's wearing is now covering my hands. It's just wet dirt, I remind myself—part of the earth beneath my boots. And somehow, my hands on her hips feel just as natural as that. "What do you say we get you home before you take another spill?"

Gemma laughs softly as her grip becomes more relaxed. Natural. Like my arms were built to have her hands resting on them. "You losing your faith in me?"

It's like her eyes hold some power over me, and I can't tear my eyes away. She's so close that it's hard not to kiss her right now. To pull her close and hold her like I want to. Even if I shouldn't. "I'd never do that."

Gemma's playful expression turns serious, and her eyes have a longing that looks like it's been there forever. My heart races when she moves in closer.

All I want to do is close the distance between us and act out on every desire that flashes through my mind. Then, a new thought crosses my mind. One that trumps all the rest and sends a tidal wave of guilt in my direction. *This is trouble.*

Trouble. There's that word again.

I draw back and clear my throat. "Let's head back."

Gemma blinks away a look of surprise and drops her eyes, nodding as she lets go of my arm. She makes a beeline to Sunshine, while I stand by wondering when I'll learn to quit putting my foot in my mouth.

I should feel some sort of relief for having the willpower to resist another kiss, but as we ride home in silence, all I feel is regret.

Regret for stopping something that feels so wrong in my head but right in my heart.

# Chapter Thirteen

**Gemma**

I exhale, taking one more nervous look into the bathroom mirror as multiple voices sound down the hall. When Dad suggested hosting a family reunion at the house this weekend, I thought it'd be a couple of aunts and uncles and maybe a few cousins, but it sounds like a small village in our living room as more and more arrive.

I smooth down the layers of my white satin wrap dress and adjust the long, billowy sleeves before mustering the courage to meet everyone. They already know me, but it'll be like I'm meeting them for the first time.

The moment I round the corner, I see the crowd spilling out of the living room. A handful more linger in the foyer and dining room. I spot my dad pouring an older woman a glass of wine in the dining room, and he prompts me to join them.

"There she is!" Dad announces loudly, making me want to disappear into the walls. He sets the bottle down on the dining table and puts his arm around me as several unfamiliar faces approach to greet me. "Everyone, Gemma is home. She's still recovering from the accident and trying to regain her memories. So, just be mindful."

I give Dad a grateful smile, hoping it will lessen some of the pressure already weighing me down. All of these people, mostly the older ones who sound like they might be shy of a few childhood memories themselves, have so much to say. And ask. I swear if one more of them asks, "Do you remember that time when...," I'm going to scream.

"Well, it's good to see you again, young lady. I'm your Uncle Howard from your mom's side." A lanky, older man wearing a white cowboy hat and a matching white button-down shirt comes up and takes my hand.

My mom's brother. I shake his hand, wondering if talking to him will make me feel closer to her. "It's nice to mee—see you again. Were you and my mother close?"

Uncle Howard grins and nods. "She was my older sister. She could be bossy at times, but she had a heart of gold. Cared about everyone and everything. I see a lot of her in you."

I hope he's not implying that he thinks I'm bossy. Though, Asher might agree with that part if he were here.

As I listen to him go on and on about the woman who used to sew all my clothes and sing me to sleep, I feel my mind wander in search of recognition. My imagination doesn't get to bloom for long before a woman in her forties with short, dark hair approaches.

"Gemma! Oh, you look so *beautiful*." The way she cups my cheeks and ogles makes me feel more like a toy poodle than a human being. "This is Rebecca. She's all grown up now!" The woman gestures to the young girl by her side.

I nod to Rebecca and smile politely, assuming I must have known her when she was a baby. "And you are?"

"Tammy! I'm a friend of the family," she says before abruptly tapping away on her phone screen. "See?" She holds up the phone, and shows me a picture of me holding a baby. "That's you holding Rebecca."

"Oh, wow. Yes, she's certainly grown a lot." My eyes flash to Tammy's, and I see that look that so many people have given me while waiting to see if I remember what they're talking about.

When I don't, she skips to another picture of me in what looks like my high school graduation gown. A matching blue cap rests on my head as I hold a bouquet of wildflowers against my chest. "We all knew you would do big things with your life after your mother passed, but it's good to have you back in Sugar Plum. Even under such unfortunate circumstances. You've been sorely missed."

It's still strange seeing myself in photos I should remember. No one expects me to remember my baby photos, but you'd think I would at least remember my high school graduation.

But I don't.

"You need to show her the prom dress she made!"

I turn to see a woman in her fifties approaching me, her phone already out and ready.

"Hi, sweetie. I'm your Aunt Florence from your dad's side," she says, squeezing my arm. She scrolls through her pictures and shows one of me wearing a sequined blue dress with one ruffled sleeve. "You made it from some old rag of a gown you found at the thrift store and transformed it into *that*. Every last sequin you insisted on stitching by hand!"

I laugh nervously, wishing I could remember my work in New York before the lights went out. "I don't remember making my prom dress, but I did help a friend mend a blouse at her shop."

Tammy and Aunt Florence's eyes widen, and Tammy leans in. "So, do you... *remember* making clothes?"

I shake my head. "No. But I found a few old sketchbooks and can see why I loved it so much."

Aunt Florence clicks her tongue in disappointment. "Well, that's a shame."

The words cut through my heart like a sharp pair of scissors on fine silk.

Before I can defend myself, I'm swept into another conversation with even more photos and hopeful looks to endure. Everyone *seems* nice enough with all their compliments and heartfelt memories. Still, I can't help but wonder how many of them want to be the one who somehow triggers mine to return. Maybe someone should politely remind them that this is not a contest.

"Now, you have to remember this. This was when you won first place in show jumping with Sunshine!" Aunt Betty shows a picture of me smiling in equestrian attire with a first-place trophy in my hand.

"You always were a natural!" Uncle Zachary grins at me.

Again, nothing sparks when I look at the picture. At least I looked happy, though. His words make me glad I'm riding Sunshine again, even if I'm not interested in competing.

Aunt Betty sighs. "It's a shame that nothing is helping you get your memories back. I can't imagine living like that. I'd be miserable without my memories."

I'm sure she doesn't mean to be rude, but what is she thinking? Am I really supposed to be that miserable all because I suffered some stupid brain injury? I'm back home, enjoying a relationship with my father that was practically non-existent when I lived in New York. I'm exploring my passions, both old and new. And I'm making friends here. *Real* friends.

"There's still plenty to enjoy, even without memories. I'm riding horses again. And I've started drawing—."

"But it's not the same," Aunt Betty objects, sounding as frustrated as she would if *she* were the one who'd been in an accident. "Your cousin, Laura, has pictures of you two growing up. I'll go find her."

I let out an exasperated sigh as soon as the coast is clear. Please, enough with the photos! All everyone wants to do is show me pictures of the past. Here's a thought. Maybe instead of mourning the death of everything I don't remember, why not take new pictures so I have something to remember moving forward?

Anything would be a better memory than this depressing day.

The room starts to spin with faces of smiling strangers talking about me like I'm still some estranged relative, and I escape into the hallway to catch my breath.

"I don't know why Henry thought bringing her home was a good idea. She hated this place."

"Yeah, fled to the city to be its biggest diva."

My eyes dart suspiciously in the direction of laughter coming from the staircase. Cousins maybe? Three women who look to be my age huddle together, gossiping, no doubt, in hushed whispers.

When I think no one is looking, I sneak out the front door, my eyes burning from the sting of tears I won't dare to cry—not yet, at least. I hear my father calling my name as I fly down the porch steps, but I ignore him. I ignore everyone. It's all too much.

I have no idea where I'm going as I race across the yard, grass staining my strappy white sandals and my face wet with tears so heavy they blur my vision. All I know is that I need to get away from all the people. With their expectations and their photos. And all their disappointment. It's suffocating!

"Gemma?"

I pause behind the stable at the sound of a familiar voice and suck in air as I try to catch my breath. My tear-stained face makes me want to hide until all signs of threat are gone, but just when I think the coast is clear, I hear the heavy footsteps coming around the corner.

"Gemma?! What's wrong? Did something happen?"

I shake my head and let the tears fall like rain. "I'm just so... tired."

Asher takes a cautious step toward me, then completely disarms me when he pulls me into the warmth of his arms. "Sshhhh. It's okay. You're safe. I've got you now. Just breathe."

My shoulders shake, and my crying turns into something more like a torrential downpour. We stay like this for some time. Asher petting my hair and gently kissing the top of my head as my violent sobs slowly morph into quiet convulsions.

When I pull away, I'm mortified by the massive pool of tears and other less attractive body fluids that create a dark stain on Asher's navy blue t-shirt. Not wanting to add insult to injury, I use my sleeve to wipe anything his shirt didn't already pick up from my nose.

Asher uses a finger to lift my chin and gazes deep into my eyes with the intensity of a meteor headed straight for the Earth, leaving a blaze of fire in its wake. "Talk to me, Gemma. What are you so tired of?"

The low rumble of his voice doesn't hide the tenderness behind his words.

"I'm tired of everyone expecting me to be someone I'm not so sure I am anymore. Maybe I did have a great childhood. And maybe I threw a lot of who I was away when I left for New York. Honestly, I don't know *what* I did because I still can't remember anything." I cringe when I think about how badly the old me may have hurt some of the same people I just tried so hard to escape from.

"I've spent a lot of time thinking about what kind of life I want to live, but when all I do is dwell on the past, I really *do* feel miserable. Actually living my life for today, though... now that feels like—."

"Like you're finally able to move on and be happy." Asher finishes my sentence with a wisdom his eyes tell me he's gained from experience.

"When did you get so good at understanding women?" I smile and wipe an eye with the back of my sleeve, noticing the streak of black mascara left behind on the delicate white fabric. There's no telling *what* kind of train wreck I look like now.

"Let's just say it's a lesson I had to learn for myself not too long ago."

Asher rests a hand on my shoulder, but this time, it's more than a comforting gesture. He caresses the crook of my neck, his fingertips resting on my nape like he wants to pull me closer.

My breath hitches as our eyes meet.

"I like how you are today, Gemma. I like *who* you are." Asher cups the back of my neck and pulls me closer. "Are you happy right now?"

My heart pounds in my chest as I gaze up at him, and in his arms, it feels like we're floating. "Yes."

"Then, nothing else matters."

He matters. A lot. And try as I might, I can't resist the urge any longer. I lift on my toes and press my lips against his, reveling in the feeling of his thick beard and mustache against my face.

Asher leans into the kiss, not shying away this time. I wanted to kiss him so badly when he picked me up out of the mud, but now I know this moment is the right one. The perfect one. He holds me close, even when our lips break apart, and rests his forehead against mine. I close my eyes.

"Cut out all the outside noise. Only how you feel matters."

I look back at the main house and wonder when to expect my father and the rest of the family to come looking for me. "Kinda hard to focus when it's so noisy around here all the time."

Asher purses his lips, and his eyes light up. "I think I might have a solution for that."

# Chapter Fourteen

**Asher**

It took some serious convincing, but after a long day of schmoozing and assuring Mr. Carter the exposure might do her some good, it's official. I'm taking Gemma to her first rodeo.

The PBR holds its Stockyards Showcase at Cowtown Coliseum in the Fort Worth Stockyards, and with Gemma taking more interest in Western fashion, I figure this would be the perfect opportunity to hone in on what's trending.

The timing is great, too, because Sam is back in town to watch Hazel. I can tell how much that so-called family reunion drained Gemma's battery. She deserves a weekend away from expectations and her past, and I'm more than happy to take her along with me and show her a little slice of my world.

"I can't believe we're really doing this," Gemma says, watching Sugar Plum's farewell sign as it fades in the rearview.

"I have a hunch you're going to love Fort Worth. Of all the places I've been, this one takes the cake." Gemma smiles, and I can feel her warmth radiating. When I feel the familiar slick of sweat coating the palms of my hands, I debate whether or not I want to crank up the a/c but decide against it. It's probably my nerves getting the best of me thinking about her watching me ride for the first time. No big deal, right?

What *is* a big deal is the kiss she laid on me last weekend. I already feel guilty enough about kissing her at the bar, but I'm a guy. I'm weak. I can't shake the intoxicating feeling in my chest when I think about her feeling the same way I do. Having her this close is addicting, and the thought of denying my impulses is almost unbearable. I have to face the fact that I'm growing more attached to this woman by the day.

Gemma is the first to break the silence. "So, bull riding, huh? How on Earth did you manage to get into such a sport?"

"My grandparents. They'd always take me to the Franklin Rodeo, and I remember thinking one day I wanted to be the one up on those bulls," I say bittersweetly. "There's one event for kids called Mutton Bustin'. It's where they put you on the back of a sheep and see how long you can stay on."

"And let me guess. You were a natural."

I laugh and shake my head. "I got shaken off after the first three seconds. I was humiliated. But I was also hooked. I kept coming back for more until I was good enough at it for my mom and dad to take notice and let me start competing for real."

"And now, here you are," Gemma replies with a nudge to my arm. Her expression softens. "Your parents... Are they—?"

I can hear the question in her voice without her even having to ask.

"They're still around. I try and get back home around the holidays when I can so Hazel can get to know them better, but it's been hard since my grandparents passed. They helped raise me when my folks weren't around, which was... a lot. Nashville doesn't feel the same without them around."

"How long ago did they pass?"

"Just before Hazel was born. It's a shame they never got to meet her. They'd have loved her. They'd have loved you, too."

If Gemma's at all taken back by my compliment, she doesn't let it show. She simply nods with a fixed look of compassion before going on. "I see. So.... Your parents never came to see you ride?"

"It's not that Mom and Dad weren't supportive when it came to my passions, but they worked for everything we had, and taking time off to watch me ride wasn't a luxury we could afford. When Grandad retired from the Air Force, he and Grandma bought an RV and used every dollar they saved, hauling me around to all my shows. They even helped foot the bill and paid my entry fees when times were tough."

"They sound amazing. I'm sorry for your loss."

"It's okay. And they were. I think if they could see me, they'd be proud of how far I've come. I could've stopped riding years ago, but... it helps me feel close to them."

"I think you're right there. And you're not just a great bull rider. You're an amazing father, too."

"I think I kinda like it when you shower me with compliments instead of insults."

Gemma smirks, looking out over the long stretch of highway ahead. "The law of reciprocity is amazing, isn't it?"

She reaches up to adjust the a/c vent, then rests her hand on the console. I have to fight the urge to hold it in mine. To feel her soft, milky skin beneath my layers of rough callouses. And to lace her delicate fingers through mine. Like there's nowhere else in the world they belong.

It's a long and tedious drive, and it's not until we hop on Interstate 20 in Abilene that a surge of adrenaline hits me. The closer we get to Fort Worth, the busier the road gets. We have to fight through rush hour traffic to get to the coliseum, but as soon as we reach the back parking lot, we're free to get out and stretch.

"Finally," Gemma says in a half yawn as she stretches her arms above her head, then turns to face the arena. It still has its older charm on the outside, but the inside has been refurbished to modern standards. "Are you nervous?"

"Nope." I haul my gear bag from the backseat and lead her toward the back entrance. "Just ready for another ride of a lifetime."

Gemma smiles and follows me as I get checked in inside. She gets a pass, and before I head to the back to get ready, I take her hand and lead her toward the stands that are steadily filling up with spectators. A rumble of excited chatter fills the arena, and the smell of dirt and cow manure gets my heart racing.

"I made sure to have them reserve a good seat for you." I gesture to a seat next to the aisle and close to the stalls.

Gemma traces the corners of her laminated pass with a finger and looks around nervously. "You can't stay a little longer?"

"It's almost show time. I can't bring you all the way out here to impress you and not deliver. You'll be just fine."

Gemma laughs and shakes her head at me. "You don't have to try hard to impress me."

"Well, you know me. If I'm going to do something, I'm doing it right."

Gemma smirks, and I swear I spot a glint of mischief in those emerald eyes. "That's a lot of words just to say that you don't want to hang out with me."

"Oh, you got jokes, do ya? Maybe we should swing by Hyena's after this. See if they're taking applications. Might even make us enough to spring for supper."

"What's Hyena's?"

"Comedy club." I shoot her a wink as she rolls her eyes. At this point, I'm starting to think that tormenting one another is the cornerstone of any good relationship. It keeps things interesting.

"Hilarious. You should go on after me, then. We could have breakfast for dinner with all the eggs they throw at you."

"Now, who's the natural?"

Still needing to gear up, I pat her knee and start down the bleachers before she has a chance to punch me. Then, before disappearing out of sight, I pitch one last look at the woman slowly inching her way into my heart.

I may have driven a nail into the coffin by bringing her here. I should be drawing away from her, not pulling her deeper into my world. My life. There are a few reasons why we shouldn't get any closer, but I can also think of a few more reasons why we should. If only it were that simple.

"Asher Davidson, as I live and breathe! I was wondering when you'd make your way back to Funky Town."

I slide a protective vest over my long-sleeved button-down and turn to greet a familiar voice. "Brady, what's up, man? I haven't seen you in forever!"

He holds up an arm and slaps my hand before patting me on the back. He's been in the rodeo circuit almost as long as I have, so it's not uncommon for us to occasionally cross paths. He gestures to his shoulder. "Yeah, I took a bad fall earlier this year. I dislocated my shoulder and had to wait for a few ribs to heal before they cleared me to ride again."

I wince, thinking about the first time I broke a rib. "Glad to see you're back. Try to keep that shoulder in place this time."

Brady laughs and nudges me with his elbow. "Will do. Saw you walk in with someone. That your new lady?"

I feel my face get hot. What kind of grown man blushes? "Naw, she's just a close friend. It's her first rodeo."

Brady looks at me like he wants to call my bluff but doesn't press the issue. "Well, you always put on a good show. I'm sure she'll enjoy it." He glances away when someone calls his name. "Gotta run. Good luck out there!"

"Good luck!"

On cue, the announcer's voice fills the arena. "Ladies and gentlemen, are you ready to rumble?! Up first in the men's division—riding Cyclone—he hails from Sugar Plum, Texas. Let's make some noise for Asher Davidson!"

I strap on my helmet and adjust my gloves as I approach the bucking chute, already hearing Cyclone's aggressive thumps and huffs. My heartbeat fills my ears as I climb onto the metal railing and look down at the restless bull.

"You've got a rowdy one today, Asher!" Brandon, one of the younger rodeo clowns, shouts over the announcer's voice as he tries to keep the bull steady while we wait for the horn to blow.

"Ain't nothing wrong with that!" I grip the braided rope wrapped around the bull's chest and shoulders in my right hand, hovering my left hand over the left side of my chaps. The rowdier the bull, the higher the points. All I need is eight seconds.

My eyes shift to the stands. When I catch sight of Gemma standing in the bleachers, my heart rate spikes, causing a rush of adrenaline.

Once I get situated behind the bull's shoulders with the rope gripped between my thighs, I press my spurs into the bull's sides and nod. I'm ready.

The gate flies open when the air horn blows, and the bull charges into the arena, kicking and twisting wildly. All sound around me slurs into a dull drone. I dig my spurs in, gripping the bull's sides with my thighs and holding the rope with every ounce of strength. The more Cyclone bucks, the more my body works to find its bearings.

It's all about balance, which is easier said than done in this line of work. The adrenaline keeps my body from registering pain as the bull jolts me around. *Come on, Asher. Just a little longer.* I grit my teeth, and time stands still as Cyclone rears, bucking hard to the right. My chest slams against his shoulders at an angle that knocks the wind out of me.

I'm thrown off instantly, hitting the dirt and rolling twice before landing on my back. Fighting for air, I turn my head and see Brandon and another bullfighter waving their arms for Cyclone's attention. When I find my breath, I roll onto my stomach and push up onto my feet.

It's the first time I've ridden this particular bull, but he must have a special vendetta against me because he ignores the two men in clown costumes chasing him and charges straight at me.

The first hit is the one I take when his thick skull makes contact with me, and the second is when I land flat on my back after being thrown like a rag doll. Darkness seeps into my vision, and the shocked sounds of the crowd fade away.

And this time, I don't get up.

# Chapter Fifteen

**Gemma**

"Asher!" My panicked cry is lost in a sea of shouts from the crowd as my heart threatens to hammer its way out of my chest. I rush down the bleachers and out of the stands, hoping to get to Asher as soon as possible. Is he okay? My last sight of him was when the bullfighters carried him out of the arena area, taking him past the chutes and through the back door.

I'm quick to flash my pass at anyone who holds a hand up and tries to stop me. I feel the adrenaline pulsing through my veins, and even if I didn't have a pass, I'm sure I'd find some superhuman way to push through whatever stands in my way. What if he's seriously hurt? What if he has to go to the hospital?

One terrifying scenario after the next fills my mind as I hurry down a white-walled hallway. I hear voices in a room to the left and stop to poke my head in. Asher is sitting on a metal table inside a small makeshift medical room while a paramedic shines a small light into his eyes.

He leans away from the paramedic and gives a sheepish look when he sees me. His clothes and hair are stained with dirt, but other than that, no blood or bones are popping out of places where they don't belong. "I promise I don't always wipe out like that."

I want to throw my arms around his neck and hug him until we're both senseless, but I reel back and turn to the paramedic. "Is he okay?"

The paramedic nods as he pockets his light. "He's fine. No signs of head trauma or broken bones. He'll be sore from bruising, though. He'll need plenty of rest."

"Thank you." A sigh of relief drifts from me as the paramedic leaves the room.

"You alright?"

"I should be asking you that. That looked terrifying!"

Asher smiles a little and shrugs. "Getting steamrolled by a bull wasn't the highlight of my night, but it'll take more than a sucker punch to sour my milk."

I approach with suspicion, my eyes scanning the length of his body to determine whether or not he's telling the truth. That paramedic may have cleared him, but I know how proud and obstinate Asher can be. It wouldn't surprise me one bit if he were lying about his pain.

"Gemma."

I snap out of my thoughts and meet his gaze. "What?"

"I'm okay. I swear. Are you really that worried about me?"

*Am I?*

I am. The thought of something terrible happening to him sent me into a panic I wasn't prepared for. It's a painful reminder that this stubborn adrenaline junky isn't the same annoying grump I once knew. He's more. So much more.

When we started working together, I promised myself I wouldn't get distracted by him. I knew I needed to focus on things that mattered. But what mattered to me in the past differs from what matters to me now.

Happiness isn't some distant memory I can regain if I try hard enough. It's the choice I make about the kind of life I want while moving forward.

I'm quickly learning that the more I try to find the old me, the more I find myself becoming someone new.

Someone I kind of like. Someone who likes *him*.

"What? I can't be worried about you?" I scoff lightly, hoping he doesn't see right through my casual demeanor, but Asher gives a pointed look that tells me I need to work on my poker face.

"I don't mind you being worried. I just don't want you giving up on the sport because you're too afraid to watch."

I let my eyes fall over his broad shoulders and gently rest a hand above each collarbone, monitoring his response as I gently trail my palms over his bulging shoulders, then down his biceps. He doesn't flinch or pull away when I apply pressure, which helps ease my worried mind. "I'm not going to stop watching you ride, Asher. I couldn't if I tried."

Asher keeps his hands on his thighs, but his eyes roam over me. "Good. I'll do even better next time."

"At least you made it to eight seconds," I say, my hands reaching his forearms.

"Not the kind of excitement you expected for your first rodeo, though, was it?" Asher chuckles as he watches my hands close in on his until they're resting in his palms.

"Worrying the bull gave you amnesia, too? Nope. The thought never crossed my mind." I crack a smile as another wave of relief washes over me.

Asher's eyes shift and center on a spot above my right brow. "You have a tiny scar." He reaches up with a look of concern and brushes a fingertip over the patch of raised skin, still pink from healing.

"No clue how it got there. My guess is that it's from the accident, but I wouldn't remember if it wasn't." I place a hand over his and bring it down to rest on my cheek. "Doesn't matter though. All that matters is that I'm moving forward."

Asher's eyes meet mine. "It's kind of like you've been given a fresh start."

Heaviness settles in my chest, and my throat tightens. "It's probably for the best. I don't think... people liked me after I left town."

"What do you mean?"

I shrug, wondering if there's any truth behind my logic. "I don't know. I've wanted to ask my dad why he thinks I left, but I won't risk upsetting him. All I know is that I skipped town after graduation and never bothered to call or visit since. Then, when I heard my cousins talk about what a diva I was, it made me question what kind of person I was before. Even you didn't like me when I got back to town."

"Yeah, but let's be fair. We didn't know each other yet. If I knew you then the way I know you now, I would've never said some of the things I did."

It's crazy how memories make up so much of our identity. Without mine, I feel like a blank slate, not knowing who I am or what I was like. I've had to recreate myself from scratch.

"I wish it didn't have to be so hard. I know I like who I am since coming back to Sugar Plum. But how do I move forward knowing there's a part of me somewhere that had a life outside of this? A life I've been fighting so hard to remember?"

"Do you think it's one you'd go back to if you did?" Asher asks, gently brushing my cheek with his thumb.

That's the million-dollar question. What if I liked the life I had in New York? I've been having so much fun building a life here in Sugar Plum that I forget to ask myself what I'd do if the memories came back. *If* they come back.

"Honestly, I can't answer that question. I want to be the girl who's happy with whatever she chooses. And I hate the idea of letting someone else take that away from me."

"Then that's exactly who you should be, Gemma. Because, if you ask me, she sounds like the kind of girl I'd like to meet," he says with a sly smile.

Ugh! How does this man always know what to say to make my knees weak and my toes curl? My eyes drop down to his softly fleshy lips, peeking through their frame of thick black whiskers, and all I can think about is how they feel pressed against mine. I want to kiss him so badly.

But before I have a chance, I hear the sound of boots coming down the hall. I pull away just as an older man in a black cowboy hat and a red button-down shirt appears in the doorway.

"How you doing, champ?"

Asher gives a nod. "Hey, Bill. Doc says I'm doing fine. I feel fine. The judges come back with the final results?"

"Sure did. You scored an 80. Congratulations, Son. First place."

"Get out... You're kidding!"

"Nope! Payout is in fifteen. I just came by to share the good news. Better get out there if you don't wanna miss it." Bill tips his hat to Asher, then me, before disappearing around the corner.

"Congratulations, Cowboy! I knew you had it in you!" I throw my arms around Asher's neck, and he winces a little when I squeeze him.

He chuckles when he catches his breath and hugs me back, pulling me close. It's the kind of hug you'd expect one of us to finally cave and pull away from, but neither of us does. I don't think we care at this point. "I'm glad you're here."

He whispers the words in my ear with enough heat to set the whole stadium on fire, and I have to tighten my grip so I don't fall if my knees melt. "Me too."

When we finally break, he gives me a long, drawn-out smile that I'm happy to return, then pushes to his feet. I watch the way he moves with ease, admiring how quickly his muscles respond. Like he didn't just get rammed head-on by a bull. He might even be the strongest man I know, physically and mentally.

Asher holds an arm out to me. "After the award ceremony, what do you say we grab a bite to eat and head home? I'm up for the drive if you are."

I wrap my fingers around his bicep, and my heart flutters like a helpless baby bird. I know it's not an official date or anything, but just the thought of sharing a meal and talking about my day with him feels exactly like how I would picture ending a perfect day with the perfect man.

If my life *were* perfect.

# Chapter Sixteen

**Asher**

With every day that goes by, it gets harder and harder to put distance between me and Gemma. Heck, at this point, I'm beginning to wonder why I try so hard in the first place.

Maybe it's because of everything at risk if I give in. My job. The roof over my head. My relationship with Mr. Carter.

My heart.

And that's not to mention how messy things could get for Gemma, especially when she can't make those kinds of decisions for herself. Not yet, at least. Not without all the facts.

"I'm ready!" Gemma comes bounding out of her house in a white sun dress, jean jacket, and brown cowboy boots, and I can't help but stare. Doesn't she know how much she's torturing me with those long legs and that sun-tanned skin?

Oh, man. She knows, alright.

"Joshua and Olivia are meeting us at The Smokehouse, then we'll go from there," I say, walking her to the passenger side of my truck.

Olivia and Gemma have been spending a lot of time together, which keeps me out of the dog house with Mr. Carter knowing how happy he is to have someone else chauffeur his daughter around all day. That's how the idea of the four of us hanging out together came up in the first place. I'd be lying if I said the whole arrangement doesn't give off serious double-date vibes, but as long as no one says it out loud, I can go to bed with a clear conscience.

Don't get me wrong. It's not like I don't *want* to date Gemma. But the last thing I need is for word getting back to her dad that I'm trying to woo her into giving me a shot after he put his foot down. He doesn't have to tell me twice that Gemma's off-limits. But try telling that to my heart.

"Sounds good to me," Gemma replies, our hands briefly brushing as we walk side by side. We share a smile before I get her door for her.

I offer a helping hand because it seems like the gentlemanly thing to do, but only after having a little fun first. "Nothing like some good old Texas barbecue to dirty up that pretty New York manicure."

Gemma rolls her eyes, but I can tell she's fighting back the urge to smile. She takes my hand and lets me help her up into the truck. "What? You think after sleeping in hay and getting thrown into a mud puddle that I'm gonna shy away from a little barbecue sauce? You better look who you're talking to."

Feisty is one of the many sides of Gemma I've grown to love.

But she makes a good point. She's adapted well since her move back to Sugar Plum, and I can tell she's a lot more carefree than she was, too. Maybe life in a small town is growing on her. It makes me wonder what else might be growing on her, too.

"You're tough as nails, Gemma Carter. I'll give you that."

I crank the engine and drive into town, rolling down the windows to let in the breeze.

The old Gemma would chew me out for letting the wind ruffle her hair, but not the new Gemma. The new Gemma ignores logic and all but sticks her head out the window, letting the wind blow her hair into a tornado of curls that whip around her face. "Nothing like the wind in your hair, right?"

I glance over, taking a moment to admire the free-spirited woman sitting next to me. I know she struggles with having too much pressure on her from other people, but ever since she decided to focus on the present, I swear she seems happier.

And I want her to be happy.

The Smokehouse may be the only barbecue joint in town, but I think it goes without saying that it's the only barbecue Sugar Plum needs. Once I find a parking spot, we hop out of the truck and head toward the sound of a three-piece band playing a cover of *La Grange* by ZZ Top on the patio out back.

It might not look like much from the outside with its faded blue paint job and weathered picnic tables, but with its hole-in-the-wall vibes and live music on the weekends, it's enough to put Sugar Plum on the map.

The smell of smoked meat fills the air as we squeeze through the crowded dining room and spot Joshua and Olivia waiting at a table out back.

"Geez, you guys. Took you long enough. Grab a seat, I'm starving!" Joshua says, shooting an eager smile as we sit on the bench opposite them.

"When are you *not* starving?" Olivia quips. "Don't listen to him. He's just grumpy because he got skunked on the boat today."

Gemma's lips curl back, and she squints her eyes. "You got sprayed by a skunk?!"

"No," I laugh. "She means he didn't catch any fish. It's just a saying."

"Oh. Well, how was I supposed to know?" Gemma's face turns pink, and it takes every ounce of control not to wrap her up in my arms.

*Play it cool, Asher. Not in front of our friends.*

"So, what have you two been up to? I feel like I hardly ever see you anymore."

"Maybe because *someone* has been too busy traveling and winning rodeos to come hang out with us," Olivia says with a salty expression.

"Well, in Asher's defense, he gets along with livestock a whole lot better than he does real humans."

"Ohhhh, burn!" Olivia reaches across the table and slaps Gemma a high-five, and I look to Joshua to have my back.

He shrugs. "Sorry, Bro. You're on your own with this one."

Feeling defeated, I shift my focus back to Gemma, remembering our time in Fort Worth a few weeks back and how much fun we had on our first road trip together. I still get shaken up when I think about how scared she must have felt up there in the bleachers all by herself when I took that hit. But those are hazards of the job I'm hoping she'll get used to if she sticks around.

Because I really, *really* want her to stick around.

"I'll have you know, that bull nearly ran me over," I say defensively.

"And you took it like a champ." Gemma's gotten so quick with her jabs that I can't help but feel proud to witness her transformation.

Laughter rings around the table, and spirits lift higher as we enjoy ice-cold drinks and piping-hot brisket platters all around. I can't remember the last time I enjoyed a night out with friends where I didn't feel like a third wheel.

I have Gemma to thank for that.

"So, Gemma, I heard you're making your own clothes," Joshua says while the rest of us dig into our food.

There's hardly anything better than good Texas barbecue. The meat. The homemade rubs and sauces. The sides of baked beans and fried okra with fresh pecan pie for dessert. It's heaven on a plate.

"Trying to." Gemma gives a timid smile like she's still unsure. "I've been really inspired by the clothes Olivia sells at the boutique. There's just something about Western fashion that excites me. And I love working with such bold colors and patterns. I've been reading up on what's trending in New York, and I can't find anything like it."

Despite fashion being one language I can hardly understand, I can't help but feel excited for her. I hear the passion in her voice, and even if fashion was her thing in New York, she's finally able to explore a new version of it.

We continue our meal while Olivia and Gemma dive into all the details of an upcoming fall clothing line. It's only when I break away from the conversation that I catch Joshua's suspicious glare.

Uh oh.

I keep reminding myself that staring at Gemma in public is a bad idea. Especially around people we know. And *especially* when I can't control the idiot smile plastered on my face any time she opens her mouth. Small towns make for big rumors.

"Ugh, I'm *stuffed*." Gemma wipes at the corners of her mouth with a napkin and pushes away her nearly clean plate. "Don't tell my dad, but I think I might like this better than his chicken fried steaks."

"Good. Now, I have something to hold over your head next time we ride, and you gripe about the trail I wanna take." I smile smugly, knowing her dad doesn't want his chicken fried steak dethroned by some barbecue she got in town, and she narrows her eyes.

"You wouldn't."

"You don't think so?"

Joshua's eyes dart between me and Gemma. "Sounds like you two are having a pretty good time together out there on the ranch." He looks at Olivia, and they share a smile that's easy to decipher.

"You guys know I'm not gonna take it easy on her just because she's the boss's daughter," I say cooly. "So, what's next on the agenda?"

"Oh! We should go for a walk! Oak Grove Park is so beautiful at night ever since they added more lights," Olivia suggests.

I turn to Gemma, whose knee is pressed against mine under the table like it's being drawn in by some gravitational pull. "You okay with staying out a little longer?"

"Of course. Let's do it."

Fortunately, Oak Grove Park is close enough that we're able to walk. Hazel and I always come during the day, but we've never stayed late enough to notice the string lights hanging from tree to tree that illuminate areas of grass and the concrete walking path that goes around the park.

Olivia gasps as she twirls under the lights. "It's so pretty!" She grabs Joshua's hand and tugs him down the path toward one of the larger oak trees. "Let's take a picture!"

As Gemma and I hang back and wait for them to finish, I notice the dreamy look on her face and how the lights from a nearby tree reflect hints of gold in her eyes. "Having a good time?"

"Yeah, it's nice making new memories, you know?"

"Well, you know I'm always down to help you make more," I say, trying to be subtle as I close the space between us.

"Oh yeah? Like what?"

*Like the ones where I kiss you so hard, it knocks the breath out of you. Or ones that end with the ring of your infectious laughter. Or ones where I get to hold you longer than two people who are just friends rightfully should.*

"Memorable ones."

Gemma laughs and gives me a playful shove. "Smartie."

When I place a hand on her arm to steady myself, I let it linger for a few more seconds before moving away. "Good memories. Funny ones. Exciting ones."

"We already have a few. Why stop now, right?" Gemma looks at me with eyes that make my stomach want to flip. I'm usually pretty sturdy, but she knocks me right off my axis.

But that's what happens every time I get close to her. She's my Texas tornado, and I'm just a small-town boy trying to rope the wind.

It wouldn't be as dangerous if Hazel wasn't involved. She and Gemma are close now. And that could cause even more problems down the line. What if Hazel gets attached and Gemma's memories come back, then she up and leaves back to New York? What then?

I'll tell you exactly what will happen. Hazel will have her heart broken all over again, and this time, it'll be all my fault. And that's assuming Mr. Carter is kind enough to let me keep my job after he finds out I'm dating his daughter.

My fantasy of keeping my job, making my daughter happy, and being with Gemma is at the top of a very tall mountain loaded with hazardous conditions. And even if I do decide to climb it, who says I'll be able to make it to the top?

Words rise in my throat, but I swallow them back down. "We should probably catch up with Joshua and Olivia."

Gemma's dreamy smile fades, but she nods in compliance.

Driven by instinct, I reach out and take her arm, guiding her down the path because it's a polite gesture. At least, that's what I tell myself as we head back toward our friends.

But who am I trying to kid? I reach for Gemma because, despite her grandeur, a part of me still believes I can protect her. Keep her safe. And… because the top doesn't seem so far away when she's near me.

I know I might sound crazy. And maybe I'm just asking to be knocked down. But it's no different than a bull who throws me in the dirt.

I always find a way to get up, dust myself off, and return for another round.

# Chapter Seventeen

**Gemma**

"Gemma, look!"

After carefully packing a few new dresses I made into their garment bags, I turn to see Hazel posing in a knit halter tank top that I'm still working on.

The sight of Hazel posing in my knit halter tank top with pink and purple glitter from her princess t-shirt peeking from behind makes me wish I could capture this moment and put it somewhere so safe that no accident will ever threaten to take it away. "You look amazing!"

Hazel puts one hand behind her head and the other on her hiked-up waist, and I clap and cheer as she turns my bedroom floor into her own mini catwalk.

She and I have been spending a lot of time together since they put Sam's uncle in hospice, and because of all the back-and-forth traveling, I offer to help out with Hazel when Asher is on the road.

"If you'll hand me that tank top, I'll bag it up, and we can go to the boutique." I look down at the four other black garment bags lying on my bed with the other clothes I made.

Olivia invited me to bring them down to the boutique so she could put them on a rack and sell them for me. She's been over the moon about them from the pictures I've sent, but I hope she'll still like them when she sees what I've made in person. It's taken me weeks to design and make each piece, but I've enjoyed every second of it.

My hands seem to move out of instinct when making clothes, and ideas flow in and out of my head like I've been thinking about them for years. I know it must be some faint connection to my past, but I still hate that I can't remember anything.

At this point, it's hard to say if I ever will, but I suppose it wouldn't be the worst thing in the world if I don't. I'm happy right now, and I didn't even need my memories for that to happen. I needed my dad, my hobbies, my new friends, Hazel... and Asher, of course.

"Here you go," Hazel wiggles out of the top and carefully hands it to me, watching me store it on a hanger in the last garment bag.

I zip up the bag and grab the hangers of all five in one hand. "Let's go!"

Hazel bounds after me as I take her down the hall to the kitchen, where Dad enjoys a fresh glass of milk and a turkey sandwich over this morning's paper. "Hi, Mr. Carter!"

"Well, hey there, Hazel," Dad greets her with a warm smile before looking up at me. "Going to the boutique?"

I nod as an air of nervous excitement hangs overhead. "Olivia thinks they'll sell, but we'll see."

Dad sets his sandwich on the small stoneware plate in front of him and pushes out of his chair. When he crosses over to me, he places gentle hands on my shoulders and gives me an assuring look. "They'll be flying off the racks, honey. I'm proud of you for working so hard on them."

His words make a warm bubble burst in my chest. He's been so supportive of me this entire time, and I've even noticed he's been reeling back on pulling out old photos whenever he thinks of something new to share. He'll still tell me a story about the past every so often, which I don't mind, especially if it's about him and my mom, but he's gotten much better about reading me and my comfort level.

"Thanks, Dad," I say, pulling him in for a side hug.

He gives me a tight squeeze before letting go to grab the truck keys off the hook on the wall. He places them in my hand. "Drive slow."

It didn't take long for me to re-learn how to drive. And because the roads here are so quiet, I hardly ever have to worry about traffic. I get Hazel buckled into her car seat across from me and, with the garment bags folded neatly between us, hop into the driver's side to adjust the seat. "Ready?"

"Ready!"

With a smile lingering on my face, I drive to town while Hazel quietly plays games on a tablet my Dad gave her last year for Christmas. I love spending time with her, but I can't help the worry that comes with the job. It means a lot that Asher trusts me enough to look after her, and I don't want to violate that trust.

I don't want to mess up. I want a good relationship with Hazel because she makes me feel a way I'm not sure I've ever felt before.

Motherly. Protective. Proud.

I mentally shake the thoughts away and focus on finding a parking spot close to the boutique. Hazel happily volunteers to run ahead and hold the door while I lug all of my clothes inside for Olivia, who waits with an eager smile.

"*Girl!* I've been waiting all week for this," she says, laying the garment bags out on the counter. She unzips the first bag to reveal a white ruffle-tiered skirt. "O-M-G! Are you kidding? This is *so* cute!"

My face burns with anticipation as she reviews the other pieces I brought, and, much to my relief, she obsesses over each one. A part of me wonders if it's possible she's only reacting like this because we're friends, but it still means the world to me that she's so willing to sell them in her store. Sugar Plum may be a small town, but Olivia has a keen eye for fashion and a loyal following on Sugar Style's Facebook page.

Still, I'm skeptical when she tells me she can have them all sold in a matter of days. After studying what's trending in New York and fusing it with what's popular in Western wear, it's hard to know how well it'll be received by the fashion world, let alone the women of Sugar Plum. Honestly, I'd be happy if they sold out by the end of the month.

"I see you've brought a helper today. It's nice to see you again, Hazel," Olivia beams at Hazel, who bashfully hides behind me.

Taking a step back, I place an arm around her shoulder and pull her into my side. "Only Sugar Plum's *best* helper," I say, staring down at Hazel with proud eyes. "I'm surprising her with lunch today for all her hard work. What do you say, kiddo? You getting hungry?"

Hazel's eyes light up as she nods intensely. "I'm *starving!* Can we get pizza?" she says, putting her hands together in a pleading motion.

"You know what? I've been craving pizza myself." I laugh and return my eyes to Olivia. "I promised her a trip to the park later, but we'll be back later before you close for the day. Fingers crossed they'll bring in some business."

"You let me worry about bringing in the business. You two, have fun. I've got a few ideas for a new window display I'm dying to test out."

Hazel takes my hand, and Olivia sees us on our way out of the boutique, where we walk a few blocks down the street until the smell of tomato sauce and handmade crust hits our noses. Plum Pizzaria is a local, buffet-style restaurant with a friendly staff. The pizza is far from gourmet, but the salad bar is always stocked, and it's the only pizza place in town.

We each order the all-you-can-eat buffet and, after loading our plates, take a table by the front window.

"How has school been?" I ask.

"Good. I drew a picture of you and Daddy riding Scout and Sunshine." Hazel takes a large bite from a slice of cheese pizza with a look so casual it could only come from the mouth of a six-year-old who's never experienced love.

Or loss.

"Cool. I'd love to see it sometime."

"It's in my backpack! I'll show you when we get home." Hazel's eyes light up with excitement, and I remember how much she loves showing off everything she makes or finds. I even have a bowl on my nightstand designated for all the weird and wonderful rocks she's gifted me since the first night I babysat for her.

"I'd love that."

When we finish eating, I take her for an ice cream cone, and we hike down the road to spend the rest of the afternoon at Oak Grove Park before I gather enough courage to return to the boutique.

I can't help but wonder if any of my clothes sold. I know the boutique gets a decent amount of traffic around this time, but having a lot of customers doesn't guarantee my clothes will sell. Fortunately, money has never been an issue since I arrived in Sugar Plum. My ego, on the other hand... let's say it could use a little extra cushion. I need to know I can create pieces that spark joy for the people who buy them.

Because, in a way, these clothes feel like a part of me I can share with the world. A part that's tied to a past I no longer remember. And to a mother I will never know again.

I pause outside the boutique, and my heart sinks when I see the clothes in the window display. Clothes that were made by someone else. I scold myself for assuming Olivia planned on adding them to the new display but assure myself she must have found a better place to hang them inside.

I push the door open and hear the familiar bell as I let my eyes sweep around the sales floor. There are only a handful of customers in the store, and none of them have any of my clothes in their hands. In fact, I don't see my clothes *anywhere.*

"Where's *your* clothes, Gemma," Hazel asks innocently.

Oh, no. Maybe Olivia really *was* being nice. Maybe my clothes were so bad she had to hang them somewhere out of sight. A cold sweat threatens to break out on my forehead as I walk to the back, where Olivia finishes ringing someone up.

"Have a sweet day!" Olivia calls out before spotting me. Excitement breaks out across her face. "There you are! And just in time to see your last skirt walk out the door!"

My jaw drops. "Wait, what?"

Olivia nods enthusiastically. "I know, right!? I told you they'd be flying off the shelves after I posted the pictures you sent me on Facebook. It probably didn't hurt when I mentioned they were hand-made by Gemma Carter, Sugar Plum's most esteemed fashion designer, either."

I'm so stunned that I struggle to find my next words. There's no way! "Really? People liked them that much?"

"You act surprised. I told you they were amazing, Gemma. You didn't think I was saying that just to be nice, did you? I even had a few ask me to call when more are available. Looks like you're in business, assuming you're up for the task."

I nod eagerly, my mind already racing with fresh ideas. What I did before worked well, but I still want to try new styles and push myself. "Thanks for encouraging me to follow through with those designs. And for helping me sell them. Really. It means the world to me."

"Anything to help an old friend. It's good to have you back, Gem. Besides, you're a legend around here. This kind of publicity is great for business."

The idea of starting a new clothing line here in Sugar Plum has my skin tingling with excitement when I think about all the possibilities. Being the ungrateful girl who moved off to the big city and forgot all about who she was and where she came from may be my past, but it doesn't have to be my future. Not anymore. I can find success right here in the same town I've come to know and love. The town that made me.

"Well, if it's not too much trouble, I say let's go for it! I'll need to enlist some assistance from my favorite helper, though. What do you think—?" My voice cuts off when I realize that Hazel isn't beside me.

I whip around, my eyes scanning the entire store for a glimpse of her sandy blonde hair. But I don't see her! The heavy thump of my heartbeat fills my ears as heat floods my cheeks. "Do you see Hazel?"

Olivia rushes out from behind the counter and starts searching through the racks.

I check the other side of the store, my eyes starting to burn in panic. How'd she disappear so fast? How could I let this happen? I hurry to the front, prepared to tear apart this entire store to find her.

That's when the bathroom door opens, and Hazel steps out with her usual carefree expression.

I stumble and almost take out a mannequin on display on my way to her. "Oh, thank goodness you're okay!"

Hazel's eyes fall to the floor. "I had to go number two," she admits with a guilty look.

I remind myself to breathe as my heartbeat slows down. Hazel is okay. Everything's okay. "You have to tell me when you're going somewhere, okay? You really scared me."

"I'm sorry, Gemma." Hazel's frowns tugs at my heart, and it's enough to make me want to cry on the spot.

I hug her tight and close my eyes to fight back the tears. "It's okay. I'm just glad you're safe."

The last time I remember feeling this much distress was when I saw that bull hit Asher. I can feel my level of concern for them both intensify with each passing day, but it's a realization I'm unsure what to do with. Asher and I have an undeniable connection, but he's never come out and admitted to having feelings for me beyond friendship. Then again, he's never denied having feelings, either. All I have to work with are his mixed messages.

It's almost like he's holding me at arm's length. And if I had to guess why, I'd bet it's because of how complicated my life is. I have so much baggage with my amnesia that I can't imagine *any* man wanting to hang around long enough to unpack it all. Especially a man trying to raise a daughter all by himself.

Maybe, in another life, I could settle down and find the man of my dreams. And who knows? Maybe he'd want to start a family. With all this time I'm spending with Hazel, I bet I'd be a great mom.

But those aren't thoughts I can entertain anymore.

I need to keep my feet on the ground and focus on rebuilding my life—starting with my career. Then, I can become so prominent in my industry that finding a man won't matter. Because when you're that successful, who has time for love?

And if there's no time for love, there'll be no time for me to ruin someone else's life with all my problems.

# Chapter Eighteen

## Asher

I'm waiting on the steps for Gemma to finish sliding into her riding boots when early morning rays wash over the front porch.

"It's a good morning for riding," Mr. Carter says from his favorite rocking chair as he takes another swig from his coffee cup.

I glance up at Gemma from her spot on the porch swing, and she looks away as soon as our eyes meet. It's hard to resist the urge to smile every time I make her blush, but with her Dad nearby, I find a healthy dose of fear usually gets the job done.

Gemma nods in his direction on the other side of the porch as she pulls on the other boot. "It is. I'd like to stay out a little longer today if that's okay."

I clear my throat when I realize the last part was directed at me. "Of course. Whatever you want to do is fine by me."

Gemma flashes me a look that's both grateful and cautious. "Thanks. But only if you're not too tired."

"Gemma says you drove in from Waco last night. How'd you do?" Henry asks.

"Yes, sir. Placed third. I could've done better, but that bull was a tough one."

"You should see him ride," Gemma cuts in. "He's the best bull rider I know."

"I'm the only bull rider that you know."

"Maybe. But you still know how to put on a show." The glimmer in her eyes makes me wonder if she's messing with me. The last time she saw me ride, I ended face down in the dirt. Eight seconds or not, that bull was about four inches shy of getting the best of me.

"They invited me to compete in Dallas this weekend. It'll be my first time riding at the State Fair Rodeo." I shift my gaze back to Mr. Carter, who smiles so wide his eyes squint.

"That's great, Asher. I'm proud of you, son."

*Son?* That's a first.

"Won't Sam be heading back to Lubbock this weekend? I can look after Hazel if you need me to," Gemma offers.

"I think you should go to Dallas, Gemma. I can watch Hazel."

Both Gemma and I whip our heads up in surprise at her dad's offer.

"If that's okay with you, Asher."

Hazel loves Mr. Carter, so it's not like I don't trust him with her while we're gone. But I'm surprised he's suggesting Gemma go with me.

I nod curtly and try to hide the look of a kid whose parents just promised him ice cream for getting straight A's on his report card. "Fine by me. Gemma?"

Gemma leaps to her feet and rushes over to hug him and kiss his cheek. "Thank you, daddy. You *know* how much this means to me. I've been begging him to take me to Dallas for weeks now," she says, shifting her eyes to mine.

Now, I'm the one looking away.

I didn't expect to have a traveling companion, but I'm definitely not mad at the sudden turn of events. More alone time with Gemma has become one of my favorite guilty pleasures, even though I know how dangerous it can be.

"Well, I'm happy to oblige. You ready to ride?"

Gemma nods, meets me at the bottom of the porch steps, and mouths the words, "Thank you," before heading for the stable.

"Go ahead and saddle up. I'm right behind you," I say, turning to face Mr. Carter as soon as she's out of range. "I'll look after her, Sir."

"I know you will. Just like I'll be looking out for Hazel while you're gone."

The corner of my mouth curls up as we share a look that only a single dad would understand. Then, with a nod, I follow Gemma to the stable to saddle up Scout.

At this point, she outpaces me when it comes to gearing up her horse. But then again, she did learn from the best. "Whoa! Slow down, Speedy."

"Speed up, Cowboy. Don't want to get left standing in the rain." Gemma pitches a triumphant glare over her shoulder at me as she guides Sunshine out of the stable, and I chuckle to myself before climbing on top of Scout to catch up.

When Sunshine and Scout are side-by-side, they fall into a comfortable stride as we head North. "It was nice of your dad to encourage you to go with me to Dallas."

"Honestly, I'm surprised he would even consider it," Gemma admits, pulling her shoulders back and relaxing deeper into her saddle. "Every time I talk about wanting to visit, he gets this funny look on his face like…"

"Like he thinks you're gonna leave him all over again?"

Gemma frowns.

"Sorry. I just—know how he feels. There's nothing worse than watching someone you love walk out of your life and never know if you'll see them again."

I can't tell how deep a chord my words strike with her, but she is quiet for long enough that I regret ever putting a foot in my big mouth in the first place.

"I bet you'll like the State Fair. There's a giant Ferris wheel that lights up at night, and anything deep fried you can imagine, they're guaranteed to sell it." The words come out more nervous than I had hoped they would, and I'm even more uncomfortable when she laughs.

"Those are all good selling points."

Is she being sarcastic? Her smile is hard to read, and it's enough to elicit even more nervous chatter on my end. "I'll try not to embarrass myself this time, but I can't make any promises."

"No need to be embarrassed. You put on a good show. I was impressed." Gemma's look remains neutral, but coming from the woman who has a vice grip on my heart, her words are like honey to a black bear.

"Oh yeah…? *How* impressed?"

To my surprise, Gemma throws her heels into Sunshine, and they're off in a flash, leaving me and Scout behind in the dust to begin a chase that leads us deeper into the field. She cuts onto the path back to the apple orchard, and by the time we reach the tree line, all four of us are panting like dogs. After finding shade under the canopy of one of the larger trees, Gemma and I climb down to stretch our legs.

"I could use a snack right about now," Gemma says, peering up at a cluster of apples on a branch overhead. "Are they safe to eat?"

"No pesticides or anything. Just check for wormholes."

Gemma lifts onto her toes, trying to snag one off the branch, but they're still too far away. Her eyes tell me that she's about to go for Sunshine's stirrup to hoist her up, but my hand on her shoulder stops her.

"Here, I got you," I say before planting my feet, wrapping my arms around her thighs, and lifting her high into the air.

She digs her nails into my shoulders at first, but when she realizes I have a good grip on her, she laughs before plucking four ripe apples from the branch.

I carefully lower her down to the ground, my hands briefly resting on her waist to steady her. It takes a lot to step away, especially when the sweet smell of her apple shampoo hits me. So many little things make it hard to resist her.

Gemma's face is flushed. She's holding something back. But *what?*

"Thanks." She hands me an apple, then turns to feed another to each of the horses.

"My pleasure. We should come out here more."

Gemma inspects her apple and wipes it with her long sleeve before taking a bite. "Maybe Hazel will want to come, too, next time."

Guilt settles at the mention of Hazel. I'll admit, I get so excited about our rides together that it slips my mind to think about inviting another person. I always think about our rides as time alone to get to know each other better. And I guess a part of me always hoped Gemma felt the same way.

I take a seat at the base of the tree where a blanket of shade shields us from the mid-day. "You know, I really appreciate you taking her under your wing like you have. She loves hanging out with you and working on all that fashion stuff. It's all she talks about anymore."

"Hazel's a good kid. I like having her around."

Gemma's eyes drift up to the canopy, and I wish I could look deep into them to pull out whatever she's too afraid to say.

"I guess what I'm trying to say is that... I'm glad you're in her life. I'm glad you're in *both* of our lives. I know a lot of complicated, bad things happened to bring you back to Sugar Plum, but we're glad you're here. A lot of people are."

Gemma's eyes shift down to meet mine with the intensity of a blazing fire as she studies me. I can tell her emotions are running deep, but why? Is she mad at me? Maybe I said something to upset her. Or maybe she's just being ornery because I didn't let her pick the apples on her own.

Whatever it is, I'd give anything to know the right words to say. Holding her gaze, I can't help but let my eyes fall to her perfectly heart-shaped lips. Lips just begging to be kissed.

There's a slight quiver, then a long sigh before Gemma turns and starts chewing on her bottom lip.

We both lean back into the tree and like instinct, I lace my arm behind her neck to cushion her head from the rough bark. She tenses, then sinks deep into me, turning to rest her head on my chest.

We stay this way for a while. Her cuddled up in my arms. And me lost in the scent of apple blossoms. Until the want to make her mine consumes every cell in my body. Gemma deserves a man strong enough to weather all the storms that rage inside her. Someone who sees her through all the wind and rain and wants nothing more than to keep her safe from all of it.

Someone... like me.

# Chapter Nineteen

**Gemma**

I keep hearing about how everything is bigger in Texas, and when Asher and I arrive at the Texas State Fairgrounds in Dallas, I'm anything but disappointed.

After spending six hours in the truck, I've gotten all kinds of lessons about the city and its rich culture, which is a nice change after dodging him all week. Ever since our ride to the apple orchard, I can't help but feel like things are different between us. I miss the way things used to be when he was always poking fun at me. At least it kept the air light between us.

Now it's like he follows me around all day like a lost puppy begging me to pet him. And what's even worse is how nice he is all of a sudden. I'm hoping that with some time away from the ranch, things can return to normal.

Rush hour traffic is a total nightmare trying to get from one side of the city to the other. And whoever thought of the "Dallas mix-master" design must have been off his rocker. Even with GPS running, it's nearly impossible for us not to miss the exit when it's three lanes over in a grid-lock.

Fortunately, Asher drives the kind of truck that could take out any one of these tiny cars with a slight of the wheel. But that still doesn't warrant me loosening my grip on the "Oh Crap" handle.

The line of cars is just as backed up when we finally reach our exit, but at least we're down to a single lane. Once we finally reach the light and turn right, I spot a *huge* cowboy statue that must be at least 50 feet tall in the distance.

"There he is," Asher says, pointing. "Big Tex. Those are the fairgrounds just up ahead."

"Oh! And there's the Ferris wheel!" I gasp. It's even bigger than I imagined it to be. But nothing, aside from a giant observation tower, is bigger than Big Tex. "You're not afraid of heights, are you?"

"What do you think?" Asher gives a smirk that's so alluring it makes me want to forget my newfound resolve to keep him safely in the friend zone.

"Oh, right. Sorry, Mr. Fearless." I sneak a quick smile when he's looking for a place to turn, then resume my look of boredom when he turns my way.

"You know, you're awfully cute when you're pretending to be mad at me."

We enter a lot south of the coliseum reserved for staff and other personnel just in time to admire how the sun paints the sky with streaks of orange and yellow as it begins to set in the distance, then find the nearest gate inside.

It's a Friday night, and the fairgrounds are packed, as expected. With music looming in the background and crowds lined up in rows to enjoy various food and carnival-style games, it's no wonder people travel from all over to visit. Seeing everyone enjoying themselves makes me forget any anxiety that I might have had around large groups of people back home.

Until we reach the entrance of the coliseum, that is. It only takes one look at the large building and me remembering what's inside to suddenly find myself back in bleachers in Fort Worth... watching in horror as Asher gets plowed down by an animal the size of a compact car.

"Wait."

Asher pauses and turns to me, a look of concern spreading across his face as he reads my expression. "Hey, what's wrong? You okay?" He drops his bag on the floor, and in a flash, he's by my side. Wrapping a strong arm around my shoulder and whispering words into my ear so sweet they'd make any woman weak in the knees.

But not this woman. I can't let them. Even if it means building a Great Wall of China around my heart.

I give him a sheepish smile and look down at my feet. "Sorry, it's nothing."

But Asher sees through me like a favorite pair of reading glasses, gently placing a finger under my chin and lifting it until our eyes meet. "Gemma, what is it? Do you want to go home?"

The fact that he's willing to drop everything and take me back to Sugar Plum should testify of how good a man he really is. And how much he cares. It makes me want to throw my hands in the air and say screw it! What I feel for him... it's not some crush. It's something more.

"No. We can stay. I mean... I want to stay." My words feel shaky as they come out, and I find myself gripping his bicep to steady myself as I speak. "It's just my nerves from all the traffic, I think."

Asher's worried expression softens as he pulls me into a full embrace. "You sure?"

I all but melt into the warmth of his arms around me until I'm tired of fighting it. "Asher, what if you get hurt again? What if it's *worse?*" The words sting in my throat as I mutter them into his chest.

Proving he has the power to disarm me on all fronts, he cups a hand on the back of my head and gently rocks me in his arms until I'm practically purring. "I know you're scared. I get scared, too, sometimes. But bullriding is as much a mental sport as it is a physical one. I'll be careful, but we have to be strong, okay? I know how strong you are, Gemma. But that doesn't mean I want you to be the one carrying me out of this arena. I can hold my own."

A laugh breaks from me at the thought of me wheeling him out of here in a full body cast while he assures me he's fine and that it's just a few broken bones. Nothing to cry over, right?

"Besides, I *can't* get hurt. I still have to take you for a ride on the Ferris wheel."

"Oh, is *that* right?"

"Of course. Right after I fatten you up with funnel cake and beat you at a game of ring toss."

Asher's perfect smile is so infectious that I have to look away to deny him the satisfaction.

"Well, I guess we better get in there, then. Don't wanna push off a chance to see a grown man cry when he loses his first game of skeeball to a girl," I say as I take his hand. It's a move that feels overly indulgent, but so what if we're holding hands? Friends are allowed to hold hands, aren't they?

"After you." Asher holds the door to the coliseum open and keeps me so close once we're inside that I can feel the warmth of his breath on my skin.

After checking himself in and getting our passes, he sneaks an arm around my waist as he guides me down a narrow hallway toward the dressing rooms. "You have your ticket? It should say the seat number."

I nod, tightening my grip around his arm, not ready to let him go. A few women in beautifully fringed button-downs and shiny white boots brush by in a hurry as they announce the start of women's barrel racing, and even in the back hallways, we can hear the crowd's roar from all four corners of the arena.

There are a lot more people here than there were in Fort Worth. That means more competition, too. For a moment, I even find myself nervous *for* him, but I know no matter where he places, I'm already proud of Asher for making it to the event.

When we finally reach the end of the hallway, Asher twirls me around to face him and hits me with a kiss so fast and hard that I'm afraid I might forget my own name. "See you soon."

And just like that, he's gone, leaving me alone with a heart ready to pound out of my chest. So much for trying to keep him in the friend zone. The drive home may be a good time to set some clear boundaries for rules of engagement.

Once I shuffle through the crowd of people and get in my seat, I suck in a deep breath as the bull riding event starts. It looks like Asher is last, so I should have plenty of time to try to relax before he's on deck.

Or so I thought.

When I see how reactive the first few bulls are as they toss their riders around like rag dolls, I start chewing on my bottom lip until it bleeds. Throughout the event, I watch the competition get tossed around and bucked off left and right as the bullfighters work hard to protect them once they hit the dirt.

Finally, I spot Asher. Raking my fingers through my hair, I release a shaky breath as he approaches his chute, and I feel my blood pressure spike when he climbs up and prepares to lower himself onto a mammoth of a bull named Goliath.

The air rings with the opening riff of AC/DC's Thunderstruck over the loudspeakers, and the crowd goes wild as the announcer introduces Asher.

Oh, boy. Here we go.

"Last but not least, ladies and gentlemen, is Asher Davidson out of Sugar Plum, Texas! Asher's a frequent competitor in the Texas bullriding circuit and always puts on one heck of a show. But tonight, he really needs to shine if he wants to secure a spot in the final three. Let's see if he can do it!"

My hands cover my mouth as I watch him lower down onto the bull, fighting the urge to cover my eyes, too, when the airhorn blows. But I stay strong, for myself just as much as for him, and keep both eyes on the prize as the gate swings open and the clock starts. The bull rushes out, kicking its back legs and spinning in a circle.

*One.*

"Come on. Stay on," I murmur, my eyes flickering to the clock on the wall. His free hand remains high in the air to avoid touching anything and risk disqualification.

*Two. Three.*

Asher grips the rope in his right hand with all his strength, letting his body move with the bull to maintain balance.

*Four.*

Why does every second feel like an eternity? He only needs to pass eight to score.

The longer Asher holds on, the more frustrated Goliath becomes, until soon it's a battle of wills. With Goliath snorting and grunting as he rears back and bucks continuously, I'm afraid Asher might lose his grip when Goliath starts circling.

*Five. Six.*

"He's putting that boy through a spin cycle," I hear one man shout.

*Seven.*

My hands are clammy at this point, and the anticipation makes my entire body tense.

....Almost there.

*Eight!*

But he's not done yet.

I jump to my feet. "Come on, Ash! You *got* this!"

Asher leans back, and my eyes widen as Goliath kicks his hind legs high off the ground mid-spin, finally knocking Asher off balance and causing him to lose his grip.

My heart stops when he flies off the back of the raging bull.

Much to my shock *and* my relief, Asher lands on his feet, this time scrambling across the dirt until he's made it through the chute and back to safety.

Cheers and thunderous applause echo throughout the coliseum as the bullfighters chase Goliath back into his pen, and I lean back into a stretch, with fingers from both hands laced together behind my head.

*Breathe, Gemma. Asher's okay.*

But what about his score?

I turn my eyes to the screen and see four men scribbling notes on the pages in front of them. Asher says 90 is a hard score to hit, but he's done it before. Surely, he can do it again.

"Ladies and gentlemen, this just in from the judges. Asher Davidson, from Sugar Plum, Texas, takes first with a final score of... 92!"

My jaw drops as cheers and whistles explode all around me. I don't even think. I just start pushing, squeezing through the crowd, and flashing my pass as many times as I need to reach the side of the arena where Asher is taking off his helmet and stripping off his protective vest. "You did it!"

With slightly ruffled hair and a million-dollar smile, Asher drops his things on the ground and wraps his arms around me, picking me up and spinning me as I toss my arms around his neck. When he sets me down,

I start to congratulate him, but his lips suddenly press against mine. This time, much softer than before.

It only takes me a second to melt into the kiss. My eyes flutter shut as I rest my hand on the back of his neck, feeling the heat from his palm radiate as he caresses my cheek. Asher's warmth wraps around me like a blanket, and I never want this kiss to end.

Our lips softly brush a few times before he rests his forehead against mine, smiling as we both fight to catch our breaths.

"Well, did I do alright? I tried my best to take it easy on you."

I laugh and hug him tightly, already craving another kiss. "Save it for the ring toss, Cowboy."

Asher's hand glides up my back as he leans closer to my ear. "You're an amazing lady, Gemma Carter. I hope you know that."

I pull away when I see the line forming behind him. Men and women from the crowd, many holding hands with children, pour out of the bleachers and into the arena to get autographs of their favorite riders while the press snaps pictures.

"I think they're waiting for you. Go on, champ."

Asher laughs and kisses the top of my hand before turning to let everyone swarm him, his eyes still finding mine one more time until he's lost in the crowd.

The high I'm on lingers even after he's gone, but I still can't talk myself out of the talk I need to have with him on the long drive home. Asher's an amazing man. And any woman would be lucky to have him. But no more being selfish.

Tonight, we might act like lovers do. But tomorrow, we go right back to being friends.

# Chapter Twenty

**Asher**

"What in the world is *that*?"

"It's pho."

"Um... it's *fried*." Gemma turns her nose up when I wave the paper tray in front of her.

"Yeah. Fried pho. Try it."

"Isn't pho a soup? How do you *fry* soup? Or better yet... why *would* you?"

"I don't know. Because you can?" I shrug my shoulders and take a bite, letting the soupy goodness drip down my beard, then wipe it with the back of my sleeve for good measure.

"Ugh! You're a maniac," Gemma almost snorts as she shakes her head. There's a chill in the air from a cold front that blew through earlier in the week, which gives us another excuse to huddle close. You know. Just in case she needs a big, warm body wrapped around her. Kind of like a heated blanket, but extra, extra large.

I hold out another fried ball and wave it in her face. "Come on now... it's no good if it's cold."

She side-eyes me with suspicious eyes like I'm trying to poison her, then looks down at the ball.

"Go on now. It's not going to bite you back."

She finally gives in and agrees to try the fried infusion of noodles, beef, and herbs. I give it a dunk in the small cup of broth, and Gemma rolls her eyes when I insist on feeding it to her myself.

She takes a bite and, at first, blows air out of her mouth, glaring at me with anguish in her eyes. It's probably because the insides are still hot enough to burn off an entire patch of taste buds. But I wait, giving time for the flavors to really kick in until she comes back with the response I'm looking for.

It's not *quite* a When Harry Met Sally, "I'll have what she's having" moment, but when her eyes go wide, and she looks like she's about to melt into the floor, I take it as a win.

"Oh, woah! Okay... that is *seriously* so good!"

I chuckle as I watch her go through her range of emotions. "I might be a lot of things, but one thing I'm not is a man who doesn't know his food."

"I would've never guessed you to be such a foodie," she says, blotting her face with a napkin." "So... what's next?"

We casually stroll the perimeter, finishing the last of our fried pho while on the hunt for our next deep-fried concoction. But with vendors on every corner and my inability to read Gemma's mind, I'm easily distracted by all the carnival workers and screaming teenagers on the Wave Swing ride. I wonder how many people get sick on that thing in a day. "See anything that looks good yet? What are you in the mood for?"

"I kind of want something sweet, now," Gemma says once we toss the empty tray away.

"Sweet. Hmm." My eyes scan the aisle to our left and pick out the two most obvious. "Churreos or fried Texas Oatmeal Pie?"

A shocked look fills her face. "You're going to make me choose?"

I click my tongue and hold an arm out to her. "I knew you'd be good company."

She smiles and takes my arm, and we hit up both vendors, then find a metal picnic bench to sit on while we try some of each and people-watch.

"Mmmmm. It's the Churreos for me, hands down. I mean, come on. Churros with cream cheese frosting, chocolate syrup, *and* crushed Oreos. How can you beat that flavor combo?"

I pop the last bite of the fried Oatmeal Pie in my mouth, savoring the last bit of its almost overwhelming sweetness. "I don't know. This is hard to beat."

When both trays are empty, I take hers with mine and walk it to a trash can across from us. When I return, Gemma's quiet. She's leaning forward with elbows resting on her knees and eyes fixed on the floor.

"What are you doing, counting pebbles on the sidewalk?"

She lifts her head at the sound of my voice. "No. Just… thinking."

"Thinking, huh? Didn't anyone ever tell you thinking is bad for your health?"

She laughs, but it's not her usual playful laugh.

Something's up.

I want her to feel comfortable talking to me, but I don't want to push her. She's already had enough of that back home. "A penny for your thoughts?"

"Careful. I might take you to the bank with that one."

"That bad, huh?"

She shrugs and leans back, gazing up at the night sky. "Do you ever feel like you're stuck in this place where you want to be free to live your life, but because of your past, you don't always know how to move forward?"

I think about Ginny. The mother of my child. The only woman I ever gave my heart to. And the one who single-handedly beat it to a pulp with a sledgehammer. But I don't want to talk about her with Gemma. Some memories are better left in the past. "Care to elaborate?"

"I feel like the more I fall back into the fashion world, the more excuses I make for why I need to focus on my career. But what if I'm wrong?"

"What do you mean?"

"Look, I like you, Asher. And this... whatever *this* is... I'm having fun. But I don't expect anything more to come from it. And I don't want to assume you do either."

"Gemma, I—."

"Hold on. Just... let me get this out first." Silence fills the air, and I let it settle until she's ready to go on. "I know I don't remember who I used to be or why I made the choices I have in life. But I need to *know* who that person is before I feel right about bringing someone else into my life. Otherwise, who's to say I don't make the same mistakes all over again."

"Do you think moving to New York was a mistake?"

She pauses. "I don't know. What if it was?"

"You're here now, aren't you?"

"I guess. But I get so hyper-focused on my career and making a name for myself that I can see how it would keep me from letting anyone in. What if I never should have left Sugar Plum in the first place? What if I was... *running?*"

"Sounds like an awful lot of beating yourself up over the hypothetical."

"My life is just... complicated. I hurt enough people when I left the first time, Asher. And I can't risk having you and Hazel become another casualty of my poor life choices."

"You know, you and I may have more in common than either of us thought. Come on." I hop to my feet and reach out a hand, and Gemma stares at me like a wounded bird rejected by the nest. "I promise you, I'm not done listening, but I have an idea."

When she takes my hand, I lead her around the winding path and through the crowds to the nearest ticket booth.

"Asher, what are you doing?"

"You'll see." It's late enough that a lot of the family crowd has cleared out, leaving mostly adults. Which means the lines should be much shorter. When we round the corner, I stop and pull her into the line for the Ferris wheel.

She laughs. "Sneaky. Was this your plan all along?"

"Only part of it."

While we stand in line, Gemma briskly rubs her hands together, blowing air in them to warm them up, and I wrap my arms around her, pulling her close.

I know I shouldn't hold her hand. Kiss her. Hug her. I shouldn't be doing anything that might complicate things between us more than they already are, but they feel right. Having her by my side or in the stands cheering for me feels *right*.

Maybe that's where things went south with Hazel's mom, Ginny. We were both so young when we got together. We had our whole lives ahead of us. And she wanted to be right there beside me, cheering in the stands. Not at home, raising a baby all by herself. But Hazel deserved a stable home. She *still* does. Things were different before Gemma came along. I used to think the road was no place to start a family. And in a way, I thought I was protecting Hazel by keeping her away. She's still young, and I don't like the idea of her seeing me get hurt, but what about when she gets older? Will I always leave her behind for someone else to look after like my parents did with me?

The line steadily dwindles, and we finally hand over our coupons and slide into one of the passenger cars beside one another.

"I can't remember the last time I've been on one of these things," I say, fastening the lap belt across us.

"Funny, neither can I."

Gemma's smile and the way her green eyes shine in the light gets my heart racing. "One more new memory for the books, then."

When the wheel starts moving, Gemma grabs my hand with an excited smile and peers over the side, watching the world below get smaller as we ascend. "Look at this view!"

I look out across the Dallas skyline and see it lit up with activity. But the real view is the one sitting right beside me. I wrap an arm around her shoulder and pull her in.

"You know, you don't have to worry about things with me. I want you to know that."

Gemma's eyes shift to mine. "Worry—*how?*"

"What you said earlier... I know what shutting yourself off from the world so you don't repeat the same mistake twice feels like. And for a long time, I thought I was doing right by Hazel by not letting a woman get close. But then I see her around you and— Gemma, it's like you brought her back to life." My voice shakes as an unfamiliar lump forms in the back of my throat.

"Now, I'm not saying things aren't complicated because, trust me, they are for me, too. More than you know. But no matter what happens, I need you to know I'm here for you. Gah— Gemma, you've become one of my best friends." My voice breaks at that last part, and I swallow hard, pushing the burning lump down like a shot of whiskey.

With a touch as soft as cotton, Gemma wraps an arm around my neck and curls her fingers through my hair. Our eyes meet, and she smiles. Like everything is right in the world. Like there's nowhere else she'd rather be.

Time stands still up here with her. And I know it's for the best that we keep our feelings in check, but I can't help but want more of her. All of her. Even if it means turning my whole world upside down.

Our moment is cut short as our passenger car approaches the bottom. I unbuckle our lap belt and get out first, lending my hand as she steps down. Only she doesn't let go when we step away. Every part of me thinks nothing could make this night any better.

Until I hear a familiar song coming from the stage behind us.

"Come on!" I pull her hand in the direction of the music, and when we reach the stage, I look up to see an old familiar face. "I know this guy! I saw him play in Austin last year! You ever heard of Red Dirt Country?!"

She shoots me an expectant look, and I laugh, shrugging my shoulders.

Wade Bowen, a good ol' boy from Waco who got his start in Lubbock, is on stage finishing a song as we push through the crowd for a better view.

"He's amazing!" Gemma shouts as the last note of "Trouble" rings out.

Applause thunders around us, and we stop to watch when we find a clearing.

"Thank you! This next one is a little song I wrote called West Texas Rain. I hope y'all like it."

I hear the familiar thud of the drums followed by the strumming of the guitar and watch Gemma as she begins to sway from side to side.

*I've found a few answers.*

*I've still got questions.*

*Kept it together and fallen apart.*

"No way I'm letting this moment pass without a dance." I reach out for her hand and pull her close, our bodies moving to the beat like they were always meant to be.

Gemma smiles at me, and I keep her close, not letting an inch of space between us. I've dealt with a lot of heartache after Ginny left, but I'm tired of letting it scare me away from what's right in front of me.

My best friend. The woman I'm falling for more and more with each passing day.

*Teardrops and laughter*

*And me chasing after*

*Years that go as quick as they came*

My hand slides around to her back, the rhythm of the kickdrum beating in my chest when she brushes her fingers through the hair on the back of my head. I love it when she does that. I love everything she does.

Our love is like a dance. Slow and steady. With highs and lows.

Our eyes meet as the music surrounds us, the crowd fading away. And for a moment, it's only us and the dancefloor—the words we've shared and others we're too afraid to admit.

But look how far we've come.

*Like a West Texas rain*

I'm taken back to the time we got caught in the rain. Two strangers forced into a difficult situation. Neither of us knowing what the future had in store.

Heck, I never thought I'd be the kind of man who falls in love with the boss's daughter. That sounds more like a scene out of a bad movie than something you'd expect in real life.

But it's like Gemma said earlier. It's not wise to have expectations about what this will or won't be. One thing is for sure, though.

If I'm willing to wait for her, it's time to rip the band-aid off and ask for her father's blessing.

# Chapter Twenty-One

**Gemma**

My head is still a wreck when we get back from Dallas.

I thought things would be different after telling Asher about my fears of getting too close while still trying to sort out my life, but now it seems to have brought us even closer. What a mess.

The ranch has been quiet the last few days, with no one around. The morning after Asher and I got back into town, Sam picked up Hazel, and Dad took Asher to a cattle auction in Lubbock. They're supposed to get home later this afternoon, and while I appreciate the time to clear my head and think, the isolation is almost too much to bear.

I'm sitting at the dining room table, staring at a half-eaten piece of buttered toast, when my new cell phone rings. Dad's been hounding me for a month now to get on his plan, and while I've never been opposed to the idea, it wasn't until Olivia and I started talking business that I decided to cave.

I don't know why the idea of getting a new phone has bothered me so much until now. When they discharged me from the hospital in New York, the only thing they said they found aside from my driver's license and a couple of credit cards was a broken phone and a set of keys.

The license and the keys were helpful, at least because they helped Dad and me find my apartment. But going back wasn't much help. Most of my neighbors didn't answer their doors when we knocked, and those who did said I was very private. Even the landlord had nothing helpful to offer when Dad made arrangements to have my bills forwarded to his address.

It's like I was a ghost. And with no way for anyone I might have known to call, I figured... *what's the point?*

"Hello?"

"Gemma, hey! I'm about to close up shop for lunch. Wanna join? I'm buying."

The sound of Olivia's voice is music to my ears. "Oh my gosh, yes! I'm going stir-crazy cooped up all day. I can be ready in ten. Does that work for you?"

"Perfect! I'll see you in ten."

After a little tidying up, I slip into a fresh pair of boot-cut jeans and my favorite new pair of Ariats, then grab my keys to lock up while I wait on the porch.

When Olivia pulls up the drive in her white Tahoe, she honks at a small group of geese in the middle of the road that wandered up from the pond.

"Nice to see you rolled out the welcome wagon for me," she calls out her window.

I laugh and fly down the porch steps to meet her, and once I'm in the passenger seat, I reach across to give her a hug of thanks. "I really appreciate this. It's been a rough few days."

"Ummm.... Yeah! I figured something was up when I didn't hear from you. How was the fair? Did something happen?"

"I'll fill you in at lunch. But first, let's figure out where we want to eat."

Olivia and I settle into a booth at the Desert Rose Cafe and order two diet cokes and a large basket of onion rings while we mull over the rest of the menu.

"Alright, girl. Spill the tea. I want to know everything. How was your trip with Asher?"

"It was—Eventful." I lean in to take a sip through my straw while she eyes me suspiciously.

"Okay...?"

I look down and bury my face in my hands as I mutter out the next part. "We kissed."

"Kissed?!"

"....Again."

"*Girl!*... you have got some serious explaining to do!"

"I know, I know." The waitress comes by and drops off a basket of fresh onion rings from the fryer, and my stomach grumbles when the aroma hits my nose.

*Seriously, Gemma?* You just got caught with your hand in the cookie jar, and all you can think about is *food*?

I pick up the bottle of ketchup from the table and squirt some in the corner of the basket, then dunk a piping hot ring into it before shoving it into my mouth and savoring it like it's my last meal.

"Wait, so you guys kissed? And more than once?... *When?* And did you kiss him, or did he kiss you?"

My chewing is slower now and more deliberate as I do the math in my head. I swallow and let out a hesitant breath. "Remember the first time I came into your shop?"

"With Asher?"

"No, by myself."

"Oh. Yeah, I remember."

"Well, the night before, he took me to this bar. The High Moon Saloon."

"Oh my gosh, Joshua and I go there all the time."

I give her an exasperated look, and she shrinks back in her seat.

"Sorry... go on."

"So, that was the first time. He was teaching me how to two-step, and he had just rescued me from some drunken cowboy. Then, it just happened. He kissed me on the dancefloor."

"Good grief, Gemma, that was two months ago! Why didn't you tell me?" Olivia's eyes are wild as she asks the question, then start to relax as she goes in for an onion ring.

"Because I didn't know you back then. I mean, not like I do now."

"Fair. So what about the other times? *Is he a good kisser?*"

I smile, feeling the rush of warmth flood into my cheeks. "The second time was a few weeks after. My dad thought inviting some of the family over to get reacquainted would be a good idea, but it ended up being a total nightmare when half the town showed up in our living room. Then, when I left to get some fresh air, I ran into Asher behind the barn. That time, I kissed him."

"That's it. It's settled. You are officially *my* new hero." Olivia laughs, and I laugh, too. I don't remember what our relationship was like before I left Sugar Plum, but if it was anything like this, I'm sad I let it slip away for all these years.

"So, then you kissed him. What happened after—-" Her eyes get even wider this time. "You kissed him in Dallas. Didn't you?"

"Well, technically, he kissed me. Just after the rodeo when he won first place."

Olivia gushes. "Awwww! Just like from a scene to a movie. So are you guys an item now, or what?"

"Not exactly. It's complicated. Asher has this amazing daughter and a career. What kind of person would I be to come mess things up for him while trying to figure out my own life? Besides, he works for my Dad. Even *if* my life weren't such a train wreck, wouldn't that be weird?" Olivia purses her lips and takes another bite, leaving me desperate for her advice even though I know my words are only a half-truth.

My real fears lie in a question I don't dare say out loud. What if my memories *do* come back?

It's easy to say I want to stay in Sugar Plum and start a new clothing venture with Olivia when I have no idea what my life was like up until three months ago. But what happens if a day comes when I'm forced to choose between the life I have now and the one I spent nearly a decade building in New York?

"First of all, Henry *loves* Asher. And Hazel. If you tell him how you really feel, I can't imagine him standing in the way of something you want. You just have to decide... *Is* Asher what you want?"

The sudden rattle of my phone on the table makes Olivia and me jump, and I look down at the screen.

It's Asher.

"Gemma? Hey, your dad and I just got back to the house, but you're not here."

"Yeah. No, I— I'm at Desert Rose grabbing lunch with Olivia."

"Well, I was going to see if you didn't have any plans later, if you might want to go to the park with me and Hazel after I pick her up from school. And maybe grab some dinner after?"

"The park?" I look up at Olivia, who's giving me a thumbs up and mouthing the words *SAY YES* and *GO*. "Yeah. We can go to the park. What time are you thinking?"

"Hazel gets out in an hour. If you want, I can come pick you up at Olivia's shop after."

"Okay. We'll head that way after we wrap up here. I'll see you soon."

"See ya."

Olivia squeals when I hang up the phone. "You *have* to let me help you pick out an outfit."

"Calm down, it's just the park," I say, trying to downplay the sudden rush of butterflies in my stomach.

"Right. And it's *just* Asher Davidson. Sugar Plum's official heartthrob *and* most eligible bachelor."

After we finish our club sandwiches, Olivia pays the bill, and we walk around the corner to her shop, where she has me try on half of the outfits in the store before finding something we both agree on. Something not too dressy but not too casual, either.

"Oh, this belt, too!" She takes a brown leather belt with a rhinestone buckle from a display and hands it to me, and after I weave it through my belt loops, I take a step back to check the finished product in a mirror by the dressing room.

Not bad. I'm still wearing the same boots and jeans, but we swapped out my old sweatshirt for a lacy, burnt-orange top with blouson sleeves, a chunky wood and turquoise bracelet, and a long-beaded necklace with a Southern cross pendant.

Olivia stands behind me with her head over my shoulder, admiring her handiwork in the reflection. "Now, if this doesn't get that man's attention, I don't know what will." Olivia pokes her head over my shoulder to admire her handy work. When my eyes meet hers, she wraps her arms around me in a tight hug from behind. "Just like old times."

I expect her words to make me feel uncomfortable. But they don't.

Tears threaten to fill my eyes, and I laugh them away. "Thank you—For everything. You've been an amazing friend. More than I probably deserve."

"You deserve it, Gemma Carter. Always have. Always will."

We share a smile just as a few customers enter the store.

"Almost time," I say, looking up at the clock on the wall. "I'm gonna go outside and get some air while I wait."

"You got this, girl. Now, go rope you a cowboy."

As I step out onto Main Street, the sun is blinding, but as my eyes adjust, I'm excited to see the vendor with the apples across the street. Hoping to buy a few to take to the park, I open my clutch to see if I have any cash.

That's when I hear them. The rapid footsteps approaching quickly from behind.

"Gemma!?"

I spin on my heel, expecting to see a familiar face, but panic settles in when I can't place the man in the collared linen shirt rushing toward me. He looks strangely out of place with his hair in a quiff and his penny loafers with no socks.

"I've been looking all over for you!"

The man closes the distance between us, and I want to ask who he is and how he knows me, but I don't get a word in edgewise before his lips crash against mine in a sudden, heart-stopping kiss.

# Chapter Twenty-Two

**Asher**

"You up?"

I wake to a loud rapping on the front door and the sound of Mr. Carter's voice. I check the clock on my nightstand. It's 6:37 in the morning. I overslept.

After Gemma and I returned from Dallas yesterday afternoon, I got recruited to attend a two-day livestock auction in Lubbock this morning. Usually, Mr. Carter goes to the auctions alone, but for some reason, he asked me to ride out with him. With all the time I've been spending with his daughter, I'm not sure if confessing my love for Gemma to him on a business trip is the best idea, but I suppose it's as good of a time as any.

"Be right out."

It doesn't take more than a minute or two before I'm dressed and pulling on my boots, but I curse myself for forgetting to set an alarm. A cup of coffee right now sure would hit the spot right about now.

When I open the door, Mr. Carter is sitting in a chair on the porch with two travel mugs. "Here." He stands and hands one to me. "Gemma's been insisting on making the morning coffee and wanted me to bring this to you. Says mine's too *plain*. Whatever that means."

I give a nod and feel a bite after the first sip. "Strong," I say.

He chuckles. "Yeah, it'll put some hair on your chest, that's for sure. She ordered one of those fancy espresso machines. It just came in last week. Must be a taste she picked up in New York because I'd never heard of such a thing until she told me about it."

The idea of Gemma bringing some of that city flair back to Sugar Plum might not be such a bad thing. I could get used to waking up to her making me a fresh cup of coffee every morning.

"We might as well get an early start and beat the traffic. I'll need your help hooking up the trailers. We can grab breakfast on the road."

On the way out of town, we hit the Whataburger drive-through and order two breakfast taquitos and four breakfast-on-a-buns to soak up some of the caffeine. Talk on the hour-and-a-half drive is primarily about business, but my mind is on Gemma and how I'm going to approach such a sticky situation with the same man who writes my paychecks every week.

Fortunately, there's no time to talk when we hit Lubbock. We spend the entire day in and out of the auction house on the hunt for a good deal on a new bull and a few horses, then sign the paperwork and grab a couple of hotel rooms for the night since the bull won't be available for pick up until noon tomorrow.

The ride home is where things get interesting.

"So, I notice you and Gemma have been spending a lot more time together." Mr. Carter's tone is casual. It's almost like he's trying to make small talk, but I know better. This is it.

"Yes, Sir. She's come a long way since New York."

"You've done a fine job looking after her and helping her acclimate. I appreciate that."

I don't just want to look after Gemma. I want to cherish her, support her, and protect her. I want to love her, and I need him to know I'll always keep her best interests in mind.

"Permission to speak freely?"

"I thought that's what we were doing."

"Sir, I know you asked me to look after Gemma. And I feel like I've done a fine job honoring your wishes to help her find her way. I also know that she has a lot of emotional things she needs to work through. Things that might make it difficult for her to—."

"You can just stop right there, Son. I already know you've been seeing Gemma. Only a blind man would miss something that obvious."

His words knock me back in my seat. *He knows?* Why wouldn't he have said anything before? Wouldn't he have put a stop to it? "She's unlike anyone I've ever met, Sir. But it was never my intention to go behind your back. I *tried* to fight it. But I just don't know how to anymore."

"Do you love her?"

I stare forward at the road, feeling that old familiar itch return to the palms of my hands. "Yes. I believe I do. Now, I know she's still figuring things out, and I won't pressure her to make any decisions until she's good and ready... and that's a big *if.* But I also know it isn't right going on without your blessing. She may decide at the end of the day she only wants to be friends. I can respect that. But I'm not willing to risk losing your respect if she doesn't."

"You know, ever since she came back home, I don't think Gemma has been more herself than when she's with you."

I slowly let out the breath I'm holding as he continues.

"When the two of you started spending more time together, she looked less lost. And I'd see the way her eyes light up when you two started bickering. That's a fire I've only seen around someone she likes. Then, when I saw her start getting up an hour early and cooking breakfast before riding lessons, I knew something changed." He smiles and shakes his head.

"You know my story, Sir. And you know I'm not quick to entertain the thought of bringing another woman into my life after the last one. Especially with a daughter of my own to think about. But Gemma's different. She sees life through a different lens than you and me. I used to think nothing good could come from looking back at my past. But now I know that learning from those mistakes is the only way to grow and move on with my life. I can't do that if I'm unwilling to get back on the horse and open up to someone new."

"You got all that from my daughter, huh?"

"There's a lot to learn when I shut my big mouth and listen."

"And you know what could happen if her memories come back. How that could change things...? For all of us." He sighs, and his eyes get distant.

"I've thought about it a lot lately. That's why I don't want to pressure her. I want her to know she has my heart. And Hazel's heart, too. I started to tell her this weekend, but I can't sleep another wink knowing I've let you down."

"You didn't let me down, Asher. The heart wants what the heart wants. And your heart wants my daughter. Just like mine wanted her mother's once upon a time. But know this. If you ever break it, I know where to find you."

The rest of the ride is easy as Mr. Carter shares stories about Sharon, Gemma's mother, and how they used to sneak around until her daddy finally caught them. Then, he shared his own concerns about how Gemma getting her old memories back could affect their relationship. I want to reassure him and tell him that she would never leave Sugar Plum after the strong connections she's made, but I know I can't. The only thing either of us can trust at this point is time.

We finally get back to the house and unload the trailers, and I'm surprised to find she's not inside. I fish my phone out of my back pocket, seeing I'll need to pick Hazel up from school soon and pull up Gemma's number in my contacts.

Here goes nothing.

"Gemma? Hey, your dad and I just got back to the house, but you're not here."

"Yeah. No, I— I'm at Desert Rose grabbing lunch with Olivia."

"Well, I was going to see if you didn't have any plans later, if you might want to go to the park with me and Hazel after I pick her up from school. And maybe grab some dinner after?"

"The park…? Yeah. We can go to the park. What time are you thinking?"

"Hazel gets out in an hour. If you want, I can come pick you up at Olivia's shop after."

"Okay. We'll head that way after we wrap up here. I'll see you soon."

"See ya." I hang up the phone and let out a sigh of relief. Now, there's only one person left to talk to before my big reveal.

My thoughts only quiet down when I get to the front of the pick-up line, and Hazel climbs into the back seat of the cab. "Hey there, Sweetpea."

"Hi, Daddy," Hazel beams as one of the attendants buckles her into her car seat and shuts the door.

I drive away from the school, my heart pounding. "We're going to pick up Gemma and go to the park, okay?"

"Yay! Can she come over after? She said next time I see her, she can paint my nails."

I chuckle. "Maybe. We still have to scrounge up some dinner first. You like having Gemma around, huh?"

"Uh-huh. She's a nice lady. And she's pretty!"

"I'm glad you think so, too. How would you feel if she started coming around more?" My eyes flicker to the rearview mirror just in time to catch a confused but excited expression.

"Is she staying the night? Like a slumber party?"

"Well, it's a little different than that. Gemma is Daddy's friend, but I—."

How do I explain my feelings about the woman I love to a six-year-old?

"I was kind of hoping maybe we could be more than friends."

Hazel stares at me with a blank look on her face.

"Like, I want to ask her to go on dates." My chest grows tight the moment I let go of those words.

Hazel is quiet at first, so she's either still processing or upset.

*Please don't let her be upset.*

"Is Gemma gonna be my new mom?!" Hazel pitches in a voice loud enough to crack the windshield but only manages to leave my ears ringing.

"Oh honey, no. I mean—I *do* want Gemma to be a big part of our lives, but she doesn't even know I love her yet."

"You *love* her?!" She claps her hands and begins to chant, "Daddy and Gemma, sitting in a tree. K-I-S-S-I-N-G!"

"Alright, alright. Calm down now, Cupid." I don't know why her response surprises me. She's been practically attached to Gemma at the hip ever since the two started spending time together. Still, it's a tricky situation to navigate. Hazel's never seen me affectionate with another woman.

"So, you'd be okay if Dad asked her to be his girlfriend one day?"

Hazel looks thoughtful, but she nods. She's a smart kid, but I know the concept is probably a bit confusing. It'll be something that the three of us will figure out together with time. Assuming Gemma doesn't shoot me down first.

"We're going to pick her up, but I need you to do me a big, important favor. What I just told you is top secret. You can't tell Gemma, okay." I motion like I'm zipping my lips, locking them, and throwing away the key, and Hazel mimics my reflection from the backseat.

I park behind Olivia's Tahoe in front of Desert Rose and around the corner from her shop. A wave of nerves hit as I open the door to unbuckle Hazel. I've been thinking all day about Gemma and her possible responses. But I've never considered what might happen if I lose her as a friend.

"Daddy?" Hazel takes my hand, prompting me to look down at her. "It's okay."

Hazel's sweet voice is enough to talk me out of getting back in my truck and abandoning the mission before it even starts. "Thanks, Sweetpea." I squeeze her hand before we step onto the sidewalk.

Every step makes my heart beat faster. But something feels off, and as we approach the corner, I hear a man's voice.

"Gemma!? I've been looking all over for you!"

I round the corner with Hazel behind me to see who it is, and my heart drops when I see a stranger kissing the woman I love.

# Chapter Twenty-Three

**Gemma**

"Umm, excuse me!? What in the world are you doing?" I plant my hands on the man's chest and shove him off, and he laughs like I'm joking.

"Kissing my girlfriend, of course."

My head spins as I try to make sense of it all. This *can't* be happening. "Wait. Did you say... girlfriend?"

"Oh, come on now, Gem. You can't be mad at me still. What's *wrong* with you?"

"She has amnesia."

My heart stops at the sound of a new voice. Asher's voice.

I whip around to see him standing by the corner with Hazel peeking from behind. He looks upset, and I can feel my heart as it sinks to the pit of my stomach.

*Oh, no... they saw. They saw the kiss!*

"Asher, he kissed me. I don't even—"

"Hold on. You have amnesia?" the man asks with eyes wide.

I rake my fingers through my hair, trying to figure out what to say. And to whom. How is this happening right now? I'm torn between a man from my past who claims to be my boyfriend and the man I'm falling in love with here in Sugar Plum. "Yes, I have amnesia! I'm sorry, but I... I don't know who you are."

"This is a joke. Right? Gemma, it's me. Seth. *Your boyfriend.* We've been dating for two years," he says, cocking a brow like I should know this.

White noise fills my ears as I stare at him blankly. There's nothing about him or his appearance that I can compare to Asher's other than the fact that they both tower over me in height. Seth is much leaner, and his clothes are designer. Tailor-made, as well, if I had to guess. His hair is blonde and styled in a taper fade, trimmed in the back with longer strands blown out and styled on top. His skin is lighter, too. He doesn't have the same bridge of freckles across his nose from working out in the sun all day. Not like Asher.

He just... doesn't look like someone I'd be with.

The way he wrinkles his nose at Asher gives him a snobbish air, and I wonder if Asher saw me the same way the first time we met.

"Two years?" Asher repeats with a deep frown. He might not say it out loud, but I can tell by his look of defeat that the news is crushing. "That's a long time, Gemma."

I take a step toward Asher with pleading eyes. He can't pull away from me just because someone from my past turns up out of the blue to stake claim. This is my life, and I'm the only one who should be deciding what my next move will be.

"Look, I don't know who this guy is, but if what you're saying is true... If you really did lose your memories, we can work through it together. We have a life together back in New York. A life only I can help you remember." Seth pulls out his phone and taps around before holding it out to me.

Another picture I don't remember.

This time, it's a picture of me and Seth kissing at what looks like a New Year's Eve party. A sea of smiling faces holding sparklers and glasses of champagne surround us as he pulls me close.

He swipes endlessly, and my stomach twists with each new and seemingly happy photo of the two of us. This is the woman I was before, surrounded by the high life in my fancy clothes with all my fancy friends, attending fancy events. Maybe Asher was right about me all along.

But why should that matter now? I don't even recognize that person anymore. She's practically a stranger. After everything I've built here in Sugar Plum, shouldn't that count for something?

"See, Gemma. Look how happy you were. *We* were." When Seth places a finger below my chin and looks deep into my eyes, I search for the answers. But all I'm left with is more questions. "Let me take you home."

I tear myself away from Seth in time to see Asher pulling Hazel back as she tries to run for me. "Asher, please don't—"

"You two have a lot to sort out. We won't stand in your way. Come on, Hazel." Asher's voice is stern as he motions for her to follow him back around the corner.

I try to speak. I want to find the words to say to comfort Hazel, whose face is wet with tears as she turns away. But my eyes sting as I realize sometimes there *are* no right words. My heart aches watching the two people I've grown to love the most turn and walk away before I can tell them how much they mean to me.

But Asher is right when he says I have a lot to figure out. My worst fear is finally coming to the surface, and it's time I either sink or learn to swim.

I turn back to face Seth as he looks at all the shops with an unimpressed look. "How did you know where to find me?"

He lets out a huff. "It wasn't easy. You and I got into a bit of a lover's quarrel the last time I saw you, but it was nothing really. We all know you have your little moments when you disappear for a few days because you're stressed. An entire week passed where you weren't responding to calls or texts, and honestly, Gemma, I thought maybe you were still sulking until another week went by and no one heard from you. Luckily, Kiki's dad is a traffic cop and was able to do some digging. He told us that an accident was reported near your apartment the same night I saw you last. Said a drunk driver ran a red light and side-swiped a car at an intersection, and the woman driving was rushed to the hospital."

Dad told me I was in a car accident, but it still sends chills down my spine, knowing that two weeks went by before anyone back in New York found out about it. And what was going on in my life that would cause me to shut myself off from the world for days or even weeks at a time?

"When I finally started calling around to the hospitals, I found out you had been discharged, and all they would tell me was that a family member came and took you back home."

"And... it took you three months to finally come looking for me?"

"No one knew where to look, Gemma. You never talked about your family or where you were from besides being from Texas."

I narrow my eyes, confusion making my temples throb. I know I never called or visited my dad, but I assumed it was because things were too painful with my mother gone or that I was too busy with work to make time. That doesn't explain why I never talked about my life before New York with people I was close to, though. And it still doesn't make sense why Seth would come looking after three months have passed.

"So, going back to my original question, how did you know where to find me?" What I really want to ask is why it took him so long to come looking in the first place. Unless, of course, he stopped looking altogether.

"Come on, Gemma. You know how crazy things are for me in the months leading up to fashion week."

"No. Actually, I don't." My words come out more accusing than I had intended, but there's something about the way he's evading eye contact that makes me think there's more to the story than he's letting on to.

"Look. I know it took a long time to find you, but I knew you were with family. I figured I'd hear from you eventually, and when I didn't, I was able to get the address from your landlord. I was just stopping for coffee on my way to the hotel when I saw you leave the shop across the street. We can go over there now, and I'll explain everything."

I know caffeine is the last thing I need to calm my nerves, but a caramel macchiato does sound amazing right now.

We cross the street, and I find a table on the patio while he orders, waiting until after I take the first sip of sweet perfection before I choose my next words. "My father says I left to pursue a career in the fashion industry. Why is fashion week such a big deal for you? Did you work in the industry as well? And how did we meet?"

"I'm an event manager. We met, working on a spring fashion collective, and started dating soon after. With my connections and your talent, you and I were on track to present in London *and* Milan in the next year and a half. That's why I need you back, baby. I can't do this without you anymore."

I know I should be happy, right? New York. London. Milan. These are lifetime achievements for any designer. And it's certainly not the kind of fame I would achieve in a small town like Sugar Plum. Even if I did sell nationally, I'd need storefronts in New York and Los Angeles to be recognized by all the major players. Plus, my boyfriend of two years is finally here to take me home.

Home. There's that word again.

My smile is forced as I peer up at him.

"I should've brought you some clothes. What in the world are you wearing?" Seth's eyes sweep over my blouse, jeans, and brown cowboy boots. "Looks like you're going to a rodeo or something."

"Are you always this insulting?"

Seth blinks at me in surprise. "Sheesh, lighten up. You just don't look like... yourself."

"I happen to like my clothes". I defensively cup my hands around my coffee mug, warming them from the crisp fall air. "And I like this town."

Seth sighs and pinches the bridge of his nose. "I'm sure it has its charm, but you *belong* in New York. With me. And Kiki, Aaron, Sam, and Destiny... those are all friends waiting for you to come back. You have an amazing life, and we're ready for you to come back to it."

The thought of leaving Sugar Plum again breaks my heart, but what if Seth is right? What if the life I've always wanted is just a plane ticket away? Would I regret not going with him?

"I... I need some time to think. This is a big decision, and I might need to sleep on it for a few days before I decide."

Seth looks irritated as he pushes up from his chair. "Whenever you're serious about returning to New York, you know where to find me. You'd think there'd be more than one roach-infested hotel to choose from in this hell hole, but I guess I can give you a day to decide. Just don't take *too* long. This whole town reeks of cow manure."

There's that pretentious attitude again. If Asher ever talks to me again, I'll have to remember to apologize for ever thinking I was somehow better than him. "I'll come find you."

Seth holds my gaze for a few more seconds. "You don't belong here, Gemma. There's a reason you left and didn't come back until you didn't have a choice."

The ache that grips my chest is enough to knock the wind out of me. He's right, but I need to know the truth about why. And there's only one person who knows the answer.

Fighting back the tears in my eyes, I watch him cross the street, get into his rental car, and speed off. Why did he come crashing back into my life now of all times? I was finally ready to tell Asher that I was tired of running. And that I wanted to see where this road could take us.

But it's time to rip off the band-aid and start asking questions I've been too afraid to know the answers to before today. I pull out my phone and dial the number, letting it ring until I hear his voice on the other end.

"Dad? Can you come get me?"

# Chapter Twenty-Four

**Asher**

Joshua exits the front door of the brick house his grandfather built over thirty years ago and waves from the porch, frowning when I don't immediately get out of the truck and greet him. We've only known each other for a few years, but he knows me well enough to know something's up if I'm showing up out of the blue and unannounced.

"We're here. Want to go say hi to Marty?"

Any other day, Hazel would be flying out of the truck before I could throw it into park for a chance to play with Joshua's golden retriever. But not today. With eyes fixed on the back of the seat in front of her, her frown says it all, and I can't remember the last time she looked so sad.

The thought of Gemma choosing New York over Sugar Plum—and Seth over me—is enough to kill the both of us, and it's enough to make my heart feel like it's about to be ripped out of my chest all over again. "I know, Sweetpea. Daddy's hurting, too."

I force myself out of my truck, then walk to the passenger side to let Hazel out. It's not usually in my character to talk about my feelings with another grown man, but I know if I go back to the house, Mr. Carter will start asking questions. And right now, I need someone I trust to talk sense into me before I go home and say something I might regret to the father of the woman I love.

Once Hazel is on the porch with Marty, Joshua walks down to meet me. "What's going on, brother? You don't look so good."

My throat tightens, and I gnaw at the inside of my cheek for a minute. "It's Gemma. She... has a boyfriend back in New York. And now he's here in Sugar Plum trying to talk her into going back with him."

Despite the occasional accusation, I've never actually admitted to having feelings for Gemma to Joshua. So, it's no surprise when his look shifts from confusion to realization to disbelief as he fires round after round of questions my way.

*"Did any of her memories come back?"*

*"Does Olivia know?"*

*"Does her father know?"*

*"Do you think she's gonna go back with him?"*

*"How big of a boy is he?"*

His last question is the only one that doesn't make me feel like I've been sucker punched in the gut. If it comes down to a battle royal where the winner takes all, I know it would only be a matter of time before Gemma and I were riding off into the sunset while the skinny-jean wearing hipster cried all the way back to Times Square. But I'm afraid winning her over won't be that simple.

"I don't know who all knows yet. But she doesn't remember anything. At least, not from what I've seen. I don't know what she's going to do. I told her I'd give her space while she figures it out."

Joshua sighs and leans against my truck beside me. "Geez. I'm sorry, buddy. This whole thing is crazy. I mean, you have feelings for her, right?"

My eyes don't flinch as I stare across the field behind his house. "I love her. I was going to tell her today."

Joshua lowers his head, and there's a moment of silence before he finally speaks. "You know, Olivia and I have been around you both long enough to see there's chemistry. And heck, with the way you two fight just to turn around and make up, it's like you were made for one another. Just because some old boyfriend comes into town doesn't mean she's going to run back to New York and forget about you. That'd be like looking a gift horse in the mouth."

"But that's the problem. He's *not* an old boyfriend. He said they'd been dating for two years when she lost her memories. Then he pulled out his phone and started flashing all these pictures of them together at these big events. Even if I wanted to, it's not the kind of life a man like me could afford to offer. Why would Gemma want to give that all up for a fling with some hand she met on her daddy's ranch?"

"Boy, if you had a brain about half the size of them biceps, you'd know that girl's been crazy about you since the minute you two started butting heads. These Texas girls, man. They like a man who's not afraid to dish it right back. I think you should fight for her." Joshua gives me a nudge and offers an easy smile.

If only it were that simple.

"I can't interfere," I say as I cross my arms.

"Why not? Nothing good in life ever came without a struggle first. You don't think she's worth the fight?"

I give Joshua a look out of the corner of my eye that makes him shrink back. "Now, you, of all people, should know I don't back down from a fight if it's something worth fighting for, but don't you think she's had it hard enough? What kind of man would I be if I stomped in, professed my undying devotion, and gave her an ultimatum?"

"Kinda sounds like what this guy's doing right now, doesn't it?"

"It's *exactly* what he's doing. And because I love her, I won't make her decision any more difficult than it already is. People have been expecting things from her ever since she returned to Sugar Plum. It's time she starts making decisions for herself without worrying how it will affect everyone around her."

"You're a good man, Asher. I hope she remembers that."

Oh, I want her to remember, alright. I want her to remember our time riding to the apple orchard and dancing under neon lights. And our time together on the road to Fort Worth and at the fair in Dallas. I want her to remember those close bonds she's formed with her father, Olivia... and Hazel.

I place a hand on Joshua's shoulder. "You are, too, amigo. I take back all the bad things I ever said about you."

Joshua chuckles and nods. "I'm always here for you, brother. You know that. You and Hazel are like family. Let me know what you figure out."

I nod and slap him on the back before looking up to find Hazel rolling around in the front yard with Marty. "Come on, Sweetpea. Time to go."

Hazel and I stop at the Sonic drive-through on our way to the park for a Route 44 Dr. Pepper and a Wacky Pack, even though neither of us is in the mood to eat anything.

I think about Gemma and whether she's still with Seth or not. Or maybe Seth is back at the ranch. It's a thought that turns my stomach in a way that even twenty-three flavors can't fix.

We sit at one of the picnic tables under an oak tree in the middle of the park, and I place my hand on her back, tracing circles as she stares at her half-eaten corndog.

It almost kills me when I feel her shoulders start to shake. I pull her into my arms and brush my hand through her hair as she sobs into my side. "Shhhh. I know, baby girl. It's okay."

"Is Gemma going to leave like mom?" When Hazel pulls away and looks up at me with big, sad eyes, all I want to do is comfort her.

"I wish I knew, Sweetpea. But we have to stay strong no matter what, okay? This is hard for Gemma, too. And we want her to be happy, right?"

"But she's happy with us. I don't want her to go." More tears break from her eyes, and I pull her in close.

"I don't either. But no matter what happens, it's us against the world. Remember that."

"Maybe if you tell her you love her, she'll stay."

"I want to. Believe me, I do. But now's not the time for that. Not yet." I know it's not the answer she wants to hear, but it's the only one I have to offer. She needs to understand we can't force other people to make decisions based on how they might affect us. I tried that with Hazel's mom, and it blew up in my face.

I made her stay back after Hazel was born. It didn't seem right to have them travel all the time. Ginny and Hazel deserved the kind of home I never had growing up in a trailer park while my grandparents hauled me all over the country. So, that's what I gave them. Only, I didn't listen to what Ginny wanted. I asked her to make a decision based on what *I* thought was best for our family. Then, I left her.

Ginny was alone in a new house with a new baby while I was off chasing my dreams. I never listened to her when she tried to tell me about her dreams. So, it's no wonder she left to start a family with someone else.

And now that the tables are turned, and I know Gemma's dreams are in the fashion world, I refuse to be the one to tell her what I think she should do. If I've learned one thing from Gemma, it's that you can't go through life erasing the past and then expect not to repeat the same mistake twice. I need to know where I went wrong the first time so I can learn how to avoid messing things up with someone new.

I know I'm stubborn. It's probably my inability to look back and learn from my past that's kept me from trying to date for all these years in the first place. Gemma changed that the day she came into my life, and I'll support her no matter what she decides.

I just hope she doesn't decide that I'm the mistake she's trying to avoid.

# Chapter Twenty-Five

**Gemma**

Despite the mascara smeared across my tear-stained face, Dad doesn't ask any questions when he picks me up and drives me back to the house. I'll admit, he's gotten better about knowing how to read me when I'm not in the mood to talk about what's bothering me.

Asher and Hazel are nowhere in sight when we pull into the drive. His truck is gone, and I can't shake the feeling that he's trying to avoid me.

Not that I can blame him.

The man just saw me kissing a boyfriend I didn't even know existed.

Dad leads me into the kitchen and pulls up a chair across from me at the kitchen table. "Wanna talk about it, Peanut? I'm guessing he talked to you?"

I flash a confused look. "Who? Seth? Wait. Did you know he was here?"

"No, I was talking about Asher. Who's Seth?"

"Oh, Daddy. It was *horrible!*" My voice breaks, and I can't fight the fresh surge of tears that come as I blurt out the words and tell him everything.

I tell him about how Seth found out where I was and came looking for me and how Asher and Hazel showed up right after he decided to kiss me on the corner of Main and 5th. Then, I told him how I felt about Asher.

"I'm sorry you're hurting, Gemma. And I wish I would have known about Seth sooner. Then, maybe this whole mess could've been avoided. I feel like I let you down."

"It's not your fault. You did everything right by bringing me back here. I just don't understand why I left in the first place. He said I never even talked to him about family or where I was from. But I love it here. Did something... happen? How come I never called or came to visit?"

Finally, I'm asking the questions I've been too afraid to ask since I've been home, and all I can do is hope I'm strong enough to endure whatever answers are in store.

"Gemma, I don't know much about your life in New York City. I *wanted* to, but... watching you leave was the hardest thing I've done since losing your mom. During the last part of your senior year, we fought a lot about it. You've been dreaming of selling your clothes ever since you learned how to make them, and once you started reading all those fancy magazines, I knew it was only a matter of time before you'd go chasing after a career in the big city. But I'm your dad, Gemma. And after your mom passed, I wasn't ready to lose you, too. You were all I had left."

"Yeah, but you wouldn't have lost me, Dad. New York may be a long way from Texas, but it's only a phone call away. Maybe I was too busy to call, but didn't you ever try calling me?"

"I love you, Gemma. But that doesn't mean I'm not capable of being selfish sometimes. When you got accepted to one of the biggest fashion schools in the country, I was sore you were leaving me all alone and too proud to admit how scared I was to be in this big house all by myself. It's one of the reasons why I finally decided to hire Asher and invite him and Hazel to come live in the guest house."

He pauses and looks down at his hands, wringing them like he's trying to squeeze out the next words.

"The truth is, it wasn't you who shut off contact. It was me. I was the one too foolish to answer the phone after you left. Until, one day, you finally quit calling. I spent a lot of years angry with you for leaving, then even more angry with myself. Then, I got a call from the hospital. When they said you didn't have any memories of the past, I guess a part of me thought God was finally answering my prayers and giving us a fresh start."

Seeing the pain in my father's eyes makes me regret any decision I ever made to not fight for our relationship. Maybe it's for the best I *don't* remember.

"I wanted to tell you sooner. I hated seeing you wrestle with why you never came home to visit, but I was afraid you'd be angry with me. So angry that you'd be on the next flight to New York, and I'd lose you all over again."

"Oh, Dad!" I push back my chair and round the table, throwing my arms around him, hoping to take some of the burden he's been carrying around for all these years off his shoulders. "I'm sorry I didn't see how much you were hurting. Phone calls or not, I should've come home to check on you. But I'm here now. And there's no amount of distance I'll let keep me away for that long again."

Dad hugs me for a long time, and I can feel the weight as it lifts from our shoulders. But there's one weight that still lingers.

Seth is still waiting for an answer, and I have no idea what I want to do. "Any fatherly advice on how to handle this mess I'm in?"

"I won't lie, Peanut. You've got a big decision to make. But I want you to know that no matter what you choose, I'm ready to support you this time around. Even if you do go back, I think I'd rather have a long-distance relationship than go back to having no relationship at all. My advice is to weigh out the pros and cons, then drop a knee."

His words are as soothing as his deep, raspy tone. I imagine being a little girl and him reading me bedtime stories. "I just wish Asher would come home so I can talk to him already."

"Give him time. I'm sure he'll come around soon enough. He's got a lot on his mind he's trying to figure out, too."

With so much at stake, I guess I should be glad Asher's not around to distract me while I take a mental inventory of how each decision could play out in the long run.

If I go back to New York with Seth, there's a chance I can pick up where I left off in my career. If my name really is as big as he says it is, it's a move that could save me years of trying to rebuild a brand somewhere new.

If I stay in Sugar Plum, I'd be close to Asher and could work on rebuilding my relationship with my dad and the rest of the family. But if I did that, would anyone even notice some has-been designer trying to break back into the fashion world with Western wear made in small town, USA? Because trying to make a long-distance relationship with Asher work around our busy schedules would be too hard to do from New York, even if I do end things with Seth.

Therein lies the root of all my problems.

Do I leave Asher and Hazel behind for a guaranteed life in the spotlight? Or am I willing to put it all on the line for some fairy tale where Asher and I ride off into the sunset and live happily ever after with Hazel and my dad?

"Can I borrow the truck? I think I know what I need to do."

He fishes the set of keys from his pocket and drops them in my hand before pulling me in for a hug. "You've got this. Don't worry about anyone else. Just do what feels right in your heart, and everything else will fall into place."

"Thanks, Dad. I'll be back soon."

The drive to the Plum Tree Inn is tense, and I don't bother turning on the radio like I usually do when my head is drowning in thoughts. I need the silence to help string them all together because the conversation I'm about to have may set the trajectory for the rest of my life. I need to make it count.

When I reach the small, three-story hotel, I go to the front desk and have the attendant call Seth down to the lobby.

"That was quick. Good." The look on his face when he gets off the elevator is smug, and I wonder how any version of me could ever be attracted to someone that self-absorbed.

"Can we talk outside?"

He grimaces. "Is it still windy?"

I grind my teeth and turn for the door. Whether he follows me or not, I refuse to have this conversation in front of an audience.

I find a metal bench near the entrance out front and sit and wait until Seth finally decides to join me.

"I just want you to know you're making the right decision, Gemma. Obviously, it's good you got to come home and visit after all these years, and it's a real *shame* you lost your memories. But your fans have been waiting long enough. It's time to end this silly vacation and get back to work. And don't worry, I'll help make the transition as seamless as possible."

The audacity of his words is enough to bring me out of my seat. "Whoa, hold on, now. I never said I was ready to go back with you."

"Wh—Oh, come on, Gemma. Forget about your career for just one minute. What about us? Surely you're not still thinking of staying after seeing the kind of life we had back in New York." Seth puts an arm around my shoulder, the strong smell of leather and tobacco from his cologne burning as it hits my nose.

I pull away, instantly feeling guilty for letting one more person down. "Seth, listen. I can't go back with you. Not until I sort things out here, first."

"*Excuse* me?" He takes a step back.

"I'm sorry you came all the way out here just to hear me say that, but something happened when I lost my memories. What if I'm not the same person you knew three months ago?"

"Oh, stop being ridiculous. Do you even *hear* yourself right now? You can't possibly want to stay in this pathetic little town and give up everything you worked your entire life to achieve. I came here to take you home, and I'm not leaving without you." His words are cold, but I know there's pain beneath the surface.

"Seth—"

"No. Now, I tried to be patient with you and let you think things over, but you're obviously not thinking straight. You think you're this small-town girl who has to give up on her dreams because you went through some existential crisis, but do you really think you'll be happy here in six months when the rest of the world forgets about you?"

His words hit like shards of ice, digging into the fleshiest parts of my heart and soul. "I don't expect you to understand, and I know how painful this must be for you, too. But I *am* happy here. And I'm not so sure I'm willing to give it all up for a life I still can't remember. Maybe things would be different if I did, but that's what I need to stay and figure out."

"Babe, *please* don't do this to me… Don't do this to *us*. Trust me when I say that no one wanted the New York City dream more than you did. That's why you left this place behind the first time. You're making a name for yourself, and together, we're taking the fashion industry by storm. We're a team, Gemma. I can't do this without you."

"Well, I guess you'll have to figure it out."

Seth shakes his head and scoffs as I watch his pity party of one transform into a fit of rage.

"I'm giving you one more chance to reconsider, then, I'm leaving tomorrow. With or without you. Don't make a decision you'll live to regret because once this door shuts, it won't open again."

His theatrics are like Dr. Jeckyll and Mr. Hyde, and I'm left speechless as he storms back inside.

Feeling more confused than ever, I decide there's only one thing left to do.

It's time to tell Asher how I really feel.

# Chapter Twenty-Six

**Asher**

I love Sugar Plum. It's become my home away from home, but I don't know how easy it'll be to stay if the woman I love runs off with another man. It's like history is repeating itself all over again.

I look out the window over the kitchen sink and notice Mr. Carter's truck is gone, which probably means Gemma's still out with Seth.

And while the thought of sitting around, waiting for her to come home like some old dog with separation anxiety might sound like something only a desperate man would do, desperate times call for desperate measures.

I can't keep my mind from wondering what she's doing now. Is she out somewhere dreaming of a future back in New York? Or is she thinking about me?

Before Seth came to town, I couldn't imagine a future without Gemma in it. She was everywhere. Making me my morning cup of coffee. Helping Hazel with her math homework. Cheering me on in the stands whenever I traveled. And letting me hold her tight every night before we fall asleep together.

But now, it's like everything is dark. Maybe I need some time away.

I told Hazel to go play in her room when we got home from the park, but the house feels too quiet. I tear my eyes away from the window and head down the hall to her room, only to be greeted by more silence.

No toys clinking together. No rocks clacking. No laughter.

Feeling unsettled, I poke my head through her door to see her lying on her stomach in the middle of the floor, carefully scribbling on a piece of pink construction paper with a black Sharpie. "Whatcha doing there, Sweetpea?"

"I'm writing Gemma a letter." Her voice is determined as she continues filling the page like her life depended on it.

I crouch down next to her and place my hand on her back. "That's good, I guess. What do you want to tell her?"

Hazel tilts her head back to look at me, and I can tell by her eyes she's been crying. "I'm telling her how much we love her. So, maybe if she knows, she'll want to stay."

"That's awfully nice, but you don't have to do all that." I reach for the back of her head to give it a gentle stroke, but she jerks away before I have a chance.

"Yes, I do!" Her outburst nearly knocks me off my feet, and she stands with clenched fists and nostrils flared. "I have to do something! You won't do *anything!*"

"Whoa, hold your horses there, Cowgirl. I know you're mad. And a part of me is mad, too. What do you say we pack up some of your toys and go camping for a few days?"

Hazel stomps a foot on the ground and crosses her arms. "No! I'm not going *anywhere* without Gemma! I want Gemma!"

A part of me was hoping I had a few more good years before Hazel started going defiant on me, but now it appears that even the first-graders are joining the brigade. It must be all those hormones they're adding to the milk at school. But the other part of me sees my little girl is suffering. And that's the part that haunts my dreams at night. I let out a deep sigh.

"Listen, I need to go across the way and talk to Mr. Carter, but think about what I said. It might be good to spend a few nights under the stars. I'll even pick up some marshmallows for the campfire."

Before I leave, Hazel throws herself onto her bed and buries her face in her pillow. Her sobs are the last thing I hear when I leave the house.

The wind blows cold as I cross the field to the main house. I need to ask Mr. Carter for permission before I leave for the weekend, but given the circumstances, I don't see any reason for him to protest.

When I knock, my eyes trail to the swing on the left end of the porch, where I always see Gemma sitting with a fashion magazine in her hands. I don't know how I'll ever get along if she leaves.

Mr. Carter pulls open the door and leans against the doorframe with a concerned look. "Everything alright?"

My reply holds an equal amount of concern. "Did you talk to Gemma?"

He nods and steps back, motioning for me to come inside. "She said her old boyfriend from New York showed up in town this afternoon asking her to go back with him. I thought you were going to find her, but I guess he beat you to the punch. Then, she told me you left. It didn't sound to me like you even bothered putting up a fight."

I take a seat across from him, not expecting the conversation to take the turn it does. "With all due respect, Sir, what was I supposed to do? Throw down the gauntlet and make her choose between me and him right there on the spot?"

Mr. Carter throws back his head and lets out a chuckle. "You got some fire in you, boy. I'll give you that much. But I know you're smarter than that. Even so, she needs to know the truth about how you feel. He said his piece. Now, it's your turn. It's the only way she can make an informed decision."

"I mean, I *wanted* to tell her. But I had Hazel with me, and... I guess I panicked. And now that I've had some time to think it over, I was coming to see if you'd mind if I took Hazel camping for a few days until all this blows over."

He fixes me with a stern look. "Son, are you telling me that as soon as the earth starts to shake, you're ready to run?"

"No, Sir. I'm just looking out for my own. Hazel thinks Gemma's going to leave like her mom did, and she's really upset. When we get back, Gemma may still decide to leave for New York, but the least I can do is help take her mind off the fact."

"Sounds like running to me," he says under his breath. "I remember the first time I laid eyes on you. We were at a coffee shop in Lubbock, and you had just rolled into town with a three-year-old in tow. You couldn't ride because you didn't have steady childcare. So, you took up temp work as a hand for anyone willing to let you bring Hazel along for the day. Word around town was that you were the hardest worker anyone had seen. But I know heartache when I see it. And you had it written all over your face that day."

"Oh, I remember." I lower my eyes, picturing the day like it was yesterday.

I'd been living day-to-day and dollar-to-dollar after Ginny left, and I lost the house. My folks in Nashville would help with Hazel here and there, but I had to leave the rodeo circuit when they insisted I find a more permanent solution. That's when I got a lead on work in West Texas as a day laborer on a few bigger ranches.

When I'd get paid, it was usually enough to put us up in some cheap motel for the week, but there were times when we were sleeping in the cab of my pickup. Until I came across Mr. Carter one day in Lubbock. He asked if he could buy our breakfast, then sat and talked business while Hazel filled up on blueberry pancakes.

He said he had a friend with a daughter in school who was looking for work as a nanny and that he had an empty guest house he was looking to rent out in exchange for work around the property. I guess now, looking back, I wasn't the only one trying to mend a broken heart.

On the run, I may have been a lonesome cowboy, but Mr. Carter gave me a home in Sugar Plum and a second chance for love when I met Gemma.

"But you're not that same heartbroken young man I met that day. I can see it in your eyes. You love my daughter, and she loves you."

"Wait a minute now." His words catch me off guard. "Did she say that?"

His mouth curls up into a smile as he twists one end of his mustache. "I thought it was obvious?"

"What about Seth?"

"What about him?"

I give Mr. Carter a challenging look.

"Look, Gemma's supposed to meet with him in town now to see if anything's still there, but trust me. She's just as shaken up by him showing up out of the blue as you and I are. Things might have gone a different direction had he come looking *before* she had time to plant roots. We're not out of the fight yet."

"I just want her to be happy. No matter what she decides."

"I know you do, Son. So?" He gives an expectant look. "Are you still thinking about running, or have I talked enough sense into you to go fight for your girl?"

"I think I've done enough running."

"Then, may the best man win." Henry stands and grips my hand with a firm shake.

A surge of motivation takes hold of me as I fly down the stairs, all the words I want to say filling my mind just as fast. I may not be able to give her the life of luxury she deserves, but I can love more and better than any of the rest. I can give her my heart and the family she's always dreamed of.

I try to call Gemma first, but it goes straight to voicemail.

My next call is to Sam, who says she's free after I beg her to come by for an hour or two while I run to town.

Hazel looks less mad at the world when I tell her the news. "Where are you going?" she asks in a small voice.

"I'm going to look for Gemma."

"How come?"

"So I can tell her how much we love her."

# Chapter Twenty-Seven

**Gemma**

I'm fine until I climb into the cab of Dad's old Chevy. That's when the weight of his words come crashing around me.

Now, here I am, ugly crying in the parking lot of the Plum Tree Inn. Tears burn my eyes like a raging fire as I shrink down into my seat.

I know talking to Seth was necessary, but had I known he was such a hothead, I'd have saved myself the trouble before I agreed to meet him. He might *say* he loves me, but I just don't understand how he could be so selfish after everything I've been through.

I pull down the visor and check my mascara in the mirror before turning on the engine, wishing I had all the answers. Even if Seth and I don't work things out, what about New York and the rest of my friends? What about my career? Am I willing to throw it all away without giving it a second thought?

Doubt fills my mind as I drive back to the place I call home, wondering if... or when... all that might change.

I need to talk to Asher. If I decide not to go back to New York, I can still build a brand here in Sugar Plum and stick around so Dad doesn't have to grow old alone, but none of that sounds right if Asher and Hazel aren't in the picture.

Amid the mental chaos, I don't see the dark blue minivan rolling through the stop sign up ahead until it's right in front of me. When I slam on the brakes, my tires squeal so hard they kick up smoke. The truck screeches to a halt inches from the oncoming vehicle, and the seatbelt slams me back against the seat.

Darkness takes hold of my vision as the back of my head hits the leather with a heavy thud.

Then, light.

Then... everything.

I slowly open my eyes in a daze, my head throbbing as the dark veil over my past lifts. The first memory hits me with force, taking my breath away.

*"No! I don't want to hear it!"*

*"You're overreacting. Again. I told you I love you. What more do you want me to say?" We are in the foyer of my apartment, and Seth groans and rolls his eyes as I shove more clothes into his arms.*

*"How dare you accuse me of overreacting?" My voice trembles with a mix of hurt and anger. "All this time, I believed you actually cared about me. But no, I was just a stepping stone for your career, wasn't I? Our relationship has never been about love. You've been leveraging my reputation to boost your fashion shows this entire time!"*

*"Our shows, babe," Seth counters, his voice smooth as silk in an attempt to bridge the gap between us.*

*I raise a hand, halting him mid-step. "Don't start. I can't believe I trusted you! For two years, you've been telling everyone I'm your business partner?!"*

"Babe, come on. You're not going to trust Damian over me, are you? We're a team."

"You made me sign a contract, then stole my designs only to sell them right under my nose. What kind of person does that to a woman he loves?"

"It sounds to me like you're being a bit ungrateful. No one knew the poor, struggling designer you were before I came along. You should be thanking me for getting your foot in the door. This is what you wanted, Gemma. Fashion is your life now."

"Yeah, for now. But what happens when I'm tired, Seth? When you said you wanted to spend the rest of your life with me, I thought that meant buying a house and starting a family!"

"You can't be serious right now. Why would I ever want to trade everything we have for a house in the suburbs and a bunch of snot-nosed brats that'll grow to hate us, anyway? What you're talking about, it's... it's fashion suicide!"

"You know what? You're right. Fashion is all you've ever cared about. I was just too blind to see it. Go home, Seth. We're through."

"I'm not going anywhere!"

"Fine. Then I'll go."

"You can't leave. Where do you think you're going to go? I'm all you have."

"I'll... I'll go home!"

"The place you ran away from as fast as you could? Seriously? Whoever you think is waiting for you back home has probably already forgotten about you."

The truth of his words stings. My father and I hadn't spoken since I left Sugar Plum, but he couldn't stay angry forever. Could he?

"Have a nice life," I bite out before shoving his last pair of loafers in his arms.

*Before he can stop me, I storm out of my apartment and down to the street where my car is parked and throw myself inside, tearing down the road and away from the city as fast as I can.*

*But I don't make it.*

*My heart thumps so quickly that it's hard to breathe, and the tears that blur my vision make it impossible to see the red light I run before my car smashes into the side of a shiny red Lexus, and everything goes dark.*

I snap out of the memory with a shaky breath and rake a hand through my hair as I remember—everything. I remember my first barrel racing competition and Dad's proud smile when I hold up a first-place ribbon. I remember obsessing over the latest issues of Teen Vogue and Elle Magazine at lunch with Olivia, then skipping class to go shopping after. And I remember my mother sitting with me for hours, teaching me to read sewing patterns after school. That was before she died, and my father and I started fighting all the time.

I also remember growing annoyed with Sugar Plum. My father warned me how difficult life would be in New York, where he wasn't around to help me when I needed it. He wanted me to take a job working for the town seamstress, but there was no way I could make a *real* name for myself in a town full of nobodies. The more I immersed myself in the fashion world I read about in magazines and on the internet, the more I dreamed of a life so much bigger than the one my tiny hometown had to offer.

So, I pushed away. I applied to fashion school under Dad's nose and fought with him when he found my acceptance letter in the mail. We fought again when he found out I stole fifty dollars from his account to pay the application fee.

Looking back, I know he was trying to protect me. But at the time, it felt like he was trying to hold me back. I didn't want to listen, and I remember saying a lot of things I'd gladly pay to forget all over again if given the chance.

And though I finally made it big in the city, I lost my relationship with the only person who mattered to me. The relationships I formed after that were with shallow people who wouldn't give me the time of day if it weren't for my talent.

A honk behind me brings me back to reality, and I pull off to the side to bury my face in my hands, shame filling me whole.

How could I have ever been so selfish?

I can't answer that question, but one thing remains certain. No matter how betrayed I felt by him for cutting off contact, I never stopped loving my father. I even trusted him enough to list him as my emergency contact. That has to count for something, right?

With shaky hands, I grab my phone and call him, needing to hear his voice. Thinking about how I left him all those years ago makes me sick to my stomach, and I never want to be that self-absorbed or impulsive again.

"Peanut?"

"Dad… I'm so sorry. I'm sorry for going behind your back and applying to fashion school. And I should've never stolen that money from your account. I should've talked to you first. I'm sorry I let our differences get in the way and didn't fight harder for your forgiveness after I left." Hot tears spill down my face as fast as the words leave my mouth.

"Whoa, slow down there, Gemma." He pauses briefly, his next words sounding more puzzled than worried. "Who told you you stole money? I never—"

"I remember, Dad. I remember *everything*."

"Oh, Peanut… that's the best news I've heard all year."

It's not as great as it sounds. The shame of remembering how awful I was to him… to everyone… is nauseating.

"Are you on your way home?"

"I was. But now…I can't just yet. I need to go somewhere to clear my head. I'm sorry, Dad. I have to go." I hang up the phone before he has time to protest, and when he tries to call back, I silence my phone.

Overwhelming thoughts and feelings crash over me like a superwave, taking me deep below the surface.

I learned the hard way just how difficult moving to the big city could be for an eighteen-year-old fresh out of high school. I spent the first two years losing myself in my studies while hiding away in a dorm I could barely afford. Then, too proud to ask for help, I started taking out loans when my grant and scholarship money ran out. I missed the easiness of Sugar Plum and life at home with my dad, even if I wasn't willing to admit it.

When I finally graduated, I was at the top of my class. But I was still tens of thousands of dollars in debt and jobless. That's when I met Seth and his crew. He saw my talent immediately and promised to help launch my career into stardom. And in a lot of ways, I guess he did.

But none of that matters anymore. Sometimes, the best way to move forward is to mend what's broken from the past. And if memory serves me correctly, many relationships are left to mend—starting with one.

I pull back onto the road, letting my heart guide me back to the place where all my favorite memories reside.

# Chapter Twenty-Eight

**Asher**

I've searched every square inch of town but still find no sign of Gemma.

"Where are you?" I whisper as I drive down Main Street and past the Plum Tree Inn. My eyes sweep from side to side, hoping to catch a glimpse of her or Mr. Carter's truck. I don't understand how she's not here. Where else would she go?

My heart hammers to a sudden stop. What if she's already gone? What if Seth convinced her to leave Sugar Plum, and they're already heading to the airport?

"Oh, man..." Pain grips my chest, and a dull ringing sound fills my ears. *What if it's too late?*

Another ringing sound hits my ears. My phone. I glance down to see Mr. Carter's name and number on the screen. "Hey. Any word from Gemma?"

"Yeah, I just got off the phone with her. They're back, Son. Her memories are back."

The words come through loud and clear, but it takes my brain a moment to register them. "Wait... she *remembers*? When did this happen?"

Mr. Carter tells me about his conversation, sounding more excited than I've ever heard him sound before.

But what does this mean? How will it affect whether she stays or goes if she has her memories back?

I know I won't get any answers until I talk to her.

"I'm heading back now," I say, flipping a U-Turn at the next stop sign. "She's not here."

"What do you mean? I've been driving all over town and haven't seen her or the truck."

"I don't know where she is. She hung up before I could ask. All she said was that she needed to clear her head, then hung up. Won't answer any more of my calls."

A place to clear her head that's not the ranch and not in town.

Knowing Gemma, there's only one place she'd go to clear her head. "I think I know where to look. I'm going there now."

I end the call, and my heart races as I veer off onto an old county road heading north, driving until I see her truck. When I pull off to the side of the road and hop out of my truck, I'm greeted by the sound of wind rustling through the leaves of trees at the apple orchard.

In the distance, I make out another noise. Someone crying?

I walk deeper into the apple orchard, following the sound of sniffling until I see a familiar brown boot poking out from behind one of the trees.

"Gemma?"

Gemma leans to the side and looks around at me. "What are you doing here?"

The sight of her tear-stained cheeks shakes me. It's only been a few hours since I last saw her, but it feels like a lifetime. "Your dad told me the news. You okay?"

Gemma reaches up to wipe away tears while avoiding my eyes. "No. But I'm working on it. I was just a kid. It was foolish to think I could leave all this behind and make it on my own. I had no idea what I was getting myself into."

"That's all in the past, though. Right? You're here now."

"But it's been eight years, Asher. How do I come back from that?"

"Time means nothing unless you let it. I'm not even close to being the man I was three years ago."

"Yeah? What man was that?"

I've been too afraid to share my past with Gemma. Not because I didn't want to, but I didn't think she'd understand, and I didn't want to scare her off. "Hazel's mom left us to start a family with another man. After she had Hazel, I stopped taking her with me on the road. She wasn't very happy. She said it wasn't fair that I left her to have all the fun while she was stuck at home by herself raising our baby. But I thought I was doing right by our family."

Gemma's lips part briefly to speak, but she remains silent as I find my words.

"Eventually, she found comfort in the arms of another man. He was from a few towns over but rode in the circuit, too. He got her pregnant, then before the baby came, asked her to go on the road with him. I thought it'd kill me when she left. But it didn't. It just left me a single father trying to raise a daughter who didn't understand why her mom didn't love her anymore. After I had to quit riding to take care of Hazel, all I could think to do was pack up our bags and drive out west, hoping for something better. That's when I met your dad. He gave me a second lease on life the day he gave me work here in Sugar Plum."

"Asher, I... I'm so sorry. I didn't know."

"It's okay. I'm not telling you all this so you can feel sorry for me. I just don't want to see you lose hope in all the good things coming your way. Don't ever give up, Gemma. Not on hope and not on love."

Gemma's face softens as her lips curl into a smile. "Who said anything about love?"

"I found hope when I found Sugar Plum, but I never thought I'd find love again. Not until I found you. I love you, Gemma. I wanted to tell you earlier, but Seth showed up, and everything got messy with Hazel around. But I'm here now. I miss you. And Hazel misses you, too. And we were both wondering... if maybe you could ever see yourself... becoming a part of our family."

Another surge of tears spills down her face, and immediately I regret the part about family. She just got her memories back, and already I'm dropping another grand piano-sized decision in her lap. Nice, Asher. Real nice.

"Gemma?"

She looks up and fans her eyes, smiling through her tears. "I'm sorry. Gosh, I'm so tired of crying today."

"I'm sorry you've been crying so much. And I'm sorry for running away like I did. I never want to be the one to make you sad."

Gemma shakes her head. "Honestly, I thought about running myself. Nothing could have prepared me for what happened today. But I'm sure about two things."

My heart pounds as our eyes meet.

"One is that I can't imagine ever going back to my old life in New York."

"And the second?"

"I love you, Asher Davidson. And Hazel, too. I know there's still so much to figure out, but I can't imagine doing it without you by my side."

"So... does that mean you're here to stay?"

"What do you think?" Gemma smiles and wraps her arms around my neck, kissing me softly beneath the shade of the apple tree.

"And you're sure you won't change your mind? What about Seth?" I cup her face in my hands, looking deep into her eyes as we break apart.

She melts into my hands, wraps her fingers around my wrists, and smiles. "I'm sure. Seth isn't the man he claims to be. He only used me to get a leg up in the fashion world. In fact, I'm *pretty* sure that's the only reason he wants me to go back with him."

"Sounds like a real jerk."

"Tell me about it. Then, when I told him I needed time to think and to go on without me, can you believe he had the nerve to yell at me? He told me I had one more chance to change my mind. Like I still need time to come to my senses knowing what a slimeball he really is. Now, I'm just worried about the trouble he'll stir up if he stays any longer."

*He yelled at her?*

The thought sends a wave of anger through me, but I clench my jaw to contain it. Besides, getting all fired up isn't going to help anyone. If I want to make things easier for her, I need to stand by her side instead of getting in my head.

"Why don't we tell him to hit the road together?" I suggest.

Her face lights up. "Really? You'd do that for me?"

I press a soft kiss against her knuckles and nod. "Of course, I would. I'd do anything for you."

She leans forward and rests her forehead against mine. "I know I already said it… but I love you, Asher."

Hearing my name on Gemma's lips makes me feel strong enough to move a mountain and quick enough to outrun a wild stallion. With her, I'm invincible. But I guess that's what the love of a good woman will do to a man.

"I love you, too. I'm glad you're staying here in Sugar Plum," I say, brushing a strand of hair away from her pretty face.

"It's where I belong. Even if it took being in the wrong place with the wrong person, I guess I had to learn my lesson somehow, right?"

All my worries and fears go up in smoke, leaving me with only a smile. After all we've been through, who'd have thought the same woman who once had me hotter than a hornet now has me melting like honey?

Now, there's only one more obstacle to face. And this time, I'm not going down without a fight.

# Chapter Twenty-Nine

**Gemma**

When Asher and I head back to the hotel, I let him drive. I think I've had enough excitement behind the wheel, and now that I've gotten my memories back, I'd like to keep it that way.

It's a short but quiet drive back to town as I reflect on everything I've learned about myself. I made a lot of mistakes in the past, hurt people I love, and nearly destroyed myself for a dream I thought I couldn't achieve any other way.

So what if I won't be putting my clothes on models walking the runways of New York? At least I'll be making clothes I love for people I care about. It will be nice to help women feel good in their skin rather than selling outfits that cost more than a month's rent in a high-rise flat on the Upper East Side of Manhattan. Not to mention, I won't have to worry about any more fame monsters pretending to fall in love with me.

"Are you worried?" Asher asks, pulling into a parking space in front of the hotel. He shuts off his truck and turns to me with a look of empathy that makes my heart burst with joy.

"A little, but it's mostly nerves getting the best of me. I'm ready to be done with all of this so I can move on with my life."

Smiling, he kisses the top of my hand. "Me too."

My heart pounds like a drum as we walk into the hotel together. I know that Seth will fight me on my decision, but once he understands that I'm not backing down, I'm sure it will be the last I ever have to see of him.

After asking the desk clerk to call him back down from his room, I join Asher in the lobby and wrap my fingers around his bicep for support while we wait. Something about the way his body feels next to mine grounds me as if he were an anchor tethering me down so I don't get swept away.

Seth steps off of the elevator, and I drop my hand before he has a chance to see me hanging on Asher. The last thing I need is to cause a scene. "You're back already, I see. But, uh—." His eyes narrow at the sight of Asher. "I'm sorry. Who is this?"

"This is Asher. He's my boyfriend. My *actual* boyfriend." My voice is more shaky than I had hoped. I look up at Asher with uncertain eyes, and he places a reassuring hand on the small of my back.

Seth scoffs and crosses his arms over his chest. "Oh, I see. This is a joke, right? I thought I explained this to you already, but maybe you're not understanding. *I'm* your boyfriend, Gemma. And if this is your way of trying to get back at me for what I said earlier, then perhaps you're still just as sensitive as you were back in New York. Let's end the charades, shall we?"

Asher's hand tenses on my back, and I take his arm again, this time with a much tighter grip as I grind my teeth. Seth always finds a way to steamroll me. It's just what he does. I used to chalk it up to him being passionate and a perfectionist, but I'm through making excuses for his lousy behavior. Enough is enough.

"You really are a snake, you know that?" I half expect my eyes to fill with tears, but the adrenaline pulsing through my veins gives me the superhuman strength to resist feeling any more sadness for the man I wasted two years hoping would change.

His eyes grow wild. "What are you talking about?"

"I remember everything, Seth. I remember the last time I saw you. It was the same night of our last show when I finally learned about all the money you stole from me. I broke up with you, *remember?*"

I watch shock ripple across his face. "You never even gave me a chance to explain. Everything I did was in our best interest. It was an investment toward *our* future together."

"There *is* no future. At least, not for us. You and I want different things. You said so yourself."

"So what? You're going to throw away everything we could achieve together for—for *him?*" Seth gestures to Asher with a sour look on his face.

"Not *just* for him, Seth. Sugar Plum is my home. And I have family here... A concept I wouldn't expect someone like you to understand. I walked away from it once already, and I'm not willing to make the same mistake twice."

Seth blinks hard like he was just slapped in the face. "*Mistake?* Well, I've got news for you. You're making an even bigger mistake if you think all your hard work won't go to waste!"

"That's right—*my* hard work. You'll have to be sure to write and let me know how all those investors react when you tell them I dumped you after you scammed me out of my fair share of their money. The only thing I've *ever* wasted was the time it took to figure out what a bottom feeder you really are."

Seth grits his teeth, balling his hands into fists as his narrowed eyes dart between Asher and me. "This is ridiculous. You know what? Forget it! I'm going back to New York. Enjoy your boring life in this abysmal town!"

"Oh, I plan on it."

Seth storms off to the elevator, leaving me alone with Asher, who wears the world's proudest smile.

I wrap my arms around his neck and lean into his warmth. "I'm surprised you stayed quiet this time. A part of me expected you to swoop to my rescue."

Asher shakes his head. "What, and miss a chance to see my girl in action? Besides, from where I was standing, it didn't look like *you* were the one in need of rescuing."

"Ha!" I throw back my head and roll my eyes. "You don't think I was being too hard on him, do you?"

"Nah... But you *are* the toughest woman I know. Don't think I don't remember all the times you pointed that death stare my way. I'm just glad you weren't afraid to get a few licks in before kicking him to the curb. I'm proud of you for sticking up for yourself."

His words mean more than I could ever begin to describe. I lift on my toes and press a gentle kiss against his lips, focusing on his dazzling blue eyes and how they make my heart race. In all my years, I've never met a man that challenges me the way Asher does. It's another reason why I know he's the one for me.

The only one.

"Now, can we *please* get out of here? I miss my Dad. And Hazel."

"Let's go." Asher takes my hand and leads me out of the hotel, then tugs me along as he breaks into a full-on skip back to his truck. I swear, this man never ceases to amaze me.

When we return to the house, Dad is sitting on the front porch, carving into a piece of wood with his pocket knife.

Asher parks, shuts off the engine, and comes around to get my door. He plants a soft kiss on my forehead. "I'll leave you to it while I go round up Hazel."

I watch him go before turning just in time to see my father rushing down the steps to greet me. I throw my arms around him and press an ear to his chest, feeling the low rumble of his voice vibrate as he speaks. "I'm sorry I wasn't there for you when you needed me, Peanut."

"Don't apologize. I was never mad at you, Dad. I know you were doing the best you could after Mom passed away. I'm the one who was too stubborn to listen to anything you had to say."

"You get *that* from your old man. I'm so glad you're home."

"And for good this time. I learned my lesson the first time."

Dad places a heavy hand on my shoulder and looks deep into my eyes. "Is that really what *you* want? I don't want you hanging around just because you're worried about me."

I nod without a hint of doubt or hesitation. "I'm not worried about you, Dad. I mean, I wouldn't mind seeing you go on a date every once in a while, but I know you'd get along fine without me hogging the remote and eating up all your food. There are... other reasons I want to stay. Besides you, of course."

Dad chuckles when my eyes wander toward the guest house. "I've never seen a man light up the way he does whenever you're around. It reminds me of how I used to look at your mother."

Just then, I see Asher's front door fly open, and a small figure appears.

"Gemma! You're home!" Hazel runs so fast I'm afraid she might trip and fall as she clears the field in record time and throws herself into my arms. "I was scared you might leave."

"I'm so sorry I scared you. Being an adult is sometimes tough, but you have nothing to worry about. I'm not going anywhere."

Hazel squeezes so tight she nearly cuts off circulation. "Promise?"

"I promise. I'm staying right here where I can be close to you and your dad."

Hazel pulls back to smile at me, nodding eagerly. "And your dad, too! We can be one big, happy family."

"Forever and always," I say, giving my dad a wink as Asher joins the three of us at the bottom of the porch steps.

"What'd I miss?"

"Gemma's gonna be our family."

He looks at me with a cute smirk that makes my knees go weak. "Oh, is that right?"

"Yeah, and Henry, too!" she beams.

His eyes shift to Dad's, and the two smile at one another.

"Ummm... why do I get the feeling you two have been conspiring behind my back?" I say, eyeing them both suspiciously.

"Oh, it's nothing to worry about, Peanut. Asher knows where I keep my shotguns if he ever steps out of line."

Asher scratches the back of his head and laughs nervously. "Well, since we're all here, what do you say we fire up the pit and celebrate? To Gemma!"

"To Gemma!" Dad and Hazel chime.

The two disappear around the side of the house, and Hazel reaches up to place her tiny hand in mine. "Hey, Gemma. Want to see something cool I found behind our house?"

I nod fervently, then stumble after Hazel as she drags me toward her backyard. Smoke curls in the air as Dad and Asher get the grill going, and she shows me an interesting hole in the ground where an animal probably burrowed.

I take a moment to drink in the scene, hearing the steady murmur of Dad and Asher talking around the front about which team they think will make it to the Superbowl, and Hazel, as she recites everything she knows about the difference between venomous and non-venomous snakes.

All this time, I was looking for some missing piece to a puzzle. A clue that would show me where and how to find the secret to everlasting happiness. I used to think I could find it by traveling to exotic cities and becoming an expert in my trade. But I learned instead that real happiness isn't something you find. It's something you choose.

But if that's the case, why can't I shake the feeling of angst when I think about my decision to give up on my dreams of making it big in New York?

Or perhaps a better question would be...

If I can choose to be happy here in Sugar Plum, can I choose to be just as successful, too?

# Chapter Thirty

**Asher**

"I like this one!" Hazel's voice sounds through the door just before I can knock.

I enter the makeshift studio Mr. Carter and I built inside her mom's old garden shed, and while it still needs a fresh coat of paint on the inside, Gemma was more than surprised to find out what we've been up to this past month.

"Good. Me, too." Gemma replies. She's standing over her desk with Hazel, reviewing sketches when I step inside, and her eyes lift to meet mine. I smile and break her gaze to look around at all the walls of shelving.

It looks like a label maker threw up all over the place, but I know better than to question her methods to the madness. All I care about is that she feels like she can still work in Sugar Plum with minimal sacrifice.

"Looks good in here."

"Yeah. I still can't believe you guys did all this without me knowing."

"Your dad and I thought it was about time you had your own She-Shed. Glad to see it's working out for you."

After Gemma got her memories back a month and a half ago, I saw how much she struggled to set up a workspace in the main house. At first, she tried setting her sewing table in the back den at the main house, but without any shelving to store her supplies, the room became a moving landmine. Everywhere you turned, you were stepping over a box or tote.

Then, after Mr. Carter had enough trying to dodge them all on his way out to the garage, he asked if I would help him convert the shed for her as an early Christmas present.

I pull off my work gloves and stand near a small space heater in the corner to warm my hands from the chill outside. "How much longer before you're done for the day."

Gemma looks up from the pile of clothes on the table in front of her and brushes a strand of hair off her forehead with the back of her arm. "I don't know. I'll probably work for another few hours after Evie's mom picks up Hazel."

"Speaking of, you better go get your things all packed up before they get here. And make sure you don't forget to bring Mr. Snugbug. Gemma and I won't be able to bring him to you this time if you forget again."

"I won't forget. I'll go get him now."

"And don't forget your coat!" I call out to Hazel as she flies out of the shed. Gemma's lips curl into a smile, and she eyes me suspiciously.

"Oh, we won't, huh? Care to fill me in on the events for the evening."

"Nope. You just sit there and look pretty. I'll take care of the rest." I slip an arm around her waist and pull her into my side, feeling her warm nose nuzzle against my face.

The flowery apple blossom smell of her hair washes over me, and I wish I could hold onto her forever. I've been planning all week for tonight. Between our busy work schedules and time with Hazel, we don't get many opportunities for a romantic date night. I just hope the weather cooperates.

"Can't wait. Now, scram so I can finish up." Gemma replies.

"Take your time, and meet me at the house at sunset," I say, leaning in for a quick kiss before I go.

Once Evie's mom pulls up to the house, I walk Hazel out and hug her goodbye. "Have fun, Sweetpea."

"Bye, Dad!" Hazel hops into the car, and I buckle her in before shutting the door and sending them off.

I watch the car disappear down the drive, and my eyes shift to the sky as the sun drops. It's still cold out, but nothing a few heavy blankets and body heat won't fix. It's almost time.

I spend the next hour finishing a few chores, then hurry inside to grab everything we'll need for the night. Because the windows to Gemma's She-Shed overlook my truck, I have to be sneaky when I lug it all outside and hide it in the backseat.

I hear the door to the shed close and look up.

"I hope you're not planning on dumping my body later," she calls out. "You think you packed enough blankets back there?"

*Uh oh. Busted.*

"And here I thought *all* women wanted to date the Eagle Scout. It's cold, so you'll want to dress warm. Make sure you grab a bigger coat, too."

"So, it's something outside. Bonfire?" Her eyes are wide with curiosity, but there's no way I'm letting her guess.

"Nope. Get dressed."

She narrows her eyes at me, then leaves for the main house to get ready while I go back inside for a few more things.

After grabbing my truck keys and pulling on my tan utility jacket, I meet Gemma by the truck. My heart skips a beat when I see her. Looking as gorgeous as ever, she joins me on the passenger side in a fleece pullover and black leggings under a pair of tall, fur-lined boots.

"Hey there," I say as she hands me the down-filled coat in her hands.

Gemma cracks a laugh and shakes her head at me. "Well, hello."

"Ready?"

"I've been ready."

I hold open the door, and she climbs into the cab, but I don't take the driveway when I start the truck and throw it into drive. Tearing across the field, we ride away from the ranch until it's nothing more than a speck in the distance, and by the time the sun goes down, we can hardly make out the horizon. I park in the middle of the wispy grass under the night sky, the sound of crickets chirping all around us.

Gemma glances around with a perplexed smile. "Okay, I give up."

I chuckle and shut off the engine. I dig around in the backseat, grab an armful of blankets, and carry them to the bed of my truck, then layer by layer, I line the bed so that by the time I'm done, I'm sure it'll feel like we're lying on a cloud.

Gemma gets out, too, then watches me, her surprised features slightly illuminated by the pale moonlight.

When I lay down the last blanket, Gemma laughs. "What?"

"Did you steal that from Hazel's room?" Gemma asks as she points to the My Little Pony blanket I *absolutely* stole from my daughter's room after she left.

"Maybe," I chuckle. "You'll thank me later."

"Thank you for what? You didn't bring me all the way out here to make out in the bed of your truck, did you?"

"Not... exactly." I twist open the top of a thermos and pour piping hot chocolate into a small styrofoam cup. "I wanted to show you Leonid's," I say, passing it to her.

"Leo-who?"

"The Leonid meteor shower. It passes through every year around this time, and tonight's the peak."

"That's actually... *really* romantic," she says with eyes sparkling brighter than the stars in the sky.

"May I?" I offer a hand to hoist her up.

Once she's thrown back her hot chocolate and all but buried in a sea of blankets, I climb up to join her.

I place an arm behind her neck, and she curls up close. The sky is clear. It's the perfect night for stargazing. Then again, any night I get to spend with her is perfect.

"This is amazing," Gemma murmurs as her hand finds mine. Our fingers twine together as we admire the night sky, getting lost in our own world under a blanket of stars.

"Yeah, it is." I turn my head and meet her eyes. "I want to make a lifetime of memories with you, just like this."

Awe gleams in her eyes as she inches closer, her lips pressing against mine in a sweet kiss I don't know what a man like me ever could have done to deserve.

"I love you," she whispers.

"I love you." Words I wish I could say louder. Clearer. Words I want to shout from the top of the highest mountain.

Gemma looks up at the sky again and sighs. "The moon. It's so... beautiful."

"Hold that thought." An idea pops into my head as I push myself up and hop down from the truck bed. When I open the door to the driver's side, I flip down the visor, pull out my favorite Tracy Lawrence CD, then turn the key over and slide it into the disc tray. Because sometimes, music can speak the words that we can't find.

I hit the skip button eight times until the perfect song starts playing over the stereo.

Gemma sits up and turns to look at me knowingly. "I don't know anyone more of a romantic than you, Asher Davidson."

Leaving the door ajar, I hoist myself onto the back tire and throw my legs over the bed rail until I'm back beside the woman who taught me how to love again. I return my arm to its original position behind her neck and pull her in again. She rests her head on my chest.

She's not wrong about me being a romantic, but if she only knew that she was the reason for all of it. She's the only woman I want to spend the rest of my life winning over. Even if that means pulling out all the cheesy stops along the way.

*As you lie in my arms*
*Girl, my hearts on my sleeve*
*Words come so hard in moments like these*
*There's feelings I have that are so hard to show*
*But right now, there's one thing*
*I want you to know*

She closes the space between us, and it's like we're the same person for a moment. One soul. One heart beating.

I want her to know that I'll always love her. And that there's nothing I wouldn't do for her. Because after all we've been through together, she's the only one that would do the same for me.

*As long as the tides ebb*
*The earth turns*
*The sun sets*
*I promise I'll always be true*

"Asher."

I look down to meet her gaze, my heart ready to beat out of my chest if she keeps looking at me with those big, green eyes. I need to show her that if I want her to always be in my arms. I need to show her everything and know just how to go about it.

My lips meet hers in a soft, slow kiss as our eyes flutter shut. We lean into each other as fireworks and our own falling stars flash behind closed eyes.

What comes next might change everything, but for now, my time with her out here in the middle of the same field I fell in love with her in is all I'll ever need.

*And as long as there's stars over Texas*
*Darling I'll hang the moon for you*

# Epilogue

**Gemma**

*Eight months later*

"Pick as many as you want. I'll use the rest to make apple butter."

I watch Hazel reach up from her perch on Asher's shoulders to find another ripe apple to add to our already overflowing basket.

"Here you go, Dad," she says, dropping one into his hands.

"At the rate she's going, we might need to open up a fruit stand." Asher looks at me with a twinkle in his eye and winks. It's been a whole year since my return to Sugar Plum, and he and my father have domesticated me already.

Fortunately, my life as a thriving fashion designer is still waxing strong, so at least there's that. When an adjoining storefront next to Olivia's shop came up for rent earlier this year, I was in an excellent place to make an offer, and with the extra space, I was able to move out of the She-Shed and set up a state-of-the-art studio on Main Street.

I'm still partnered with Olivia, but we nearly doubled the sales floor, offering private label designs on one side and a custom bridal shop on the other. I never saw myself getting excited about making bridal gowns until

I moved back to Sugar Plum. But now, after opening an online storefront, I think I may have found my calling.

Once my followers from New York found out I was making dresses in Texas, the business blew up with people traveling from out of state for custom fittings.

As for things with Asher, I'm happier than I've ever been getting to be the doting girlfriend at all his shows.

"What do you say, Hazel? You wanna quit the fashion world and become a fruit vendor?" I ask.

She makes a sour face and shakes her head.

I laugh. "Good, because I'm not sure I want to lose my best apprentice."

Because school is out, Hazel rides with me to the studio and helps out most days when Asher is working on the ranch, but during the school year, Sam still helps out. Olivia and I have even started inviting Sam out when we have a girl's lunch or go shopping at the mall a few towns over. It feels so good to have *real* friends again.

The pieces of my life have finally fallen into the right place.

"What about caramel apples?" Hazel asks. This time, she pulls on an apple until it snaps off the branch, and the recoil almost sends her flying.

"Whoa, easy there, Turbo. And don't you want to wait until Summer is over and it's a little colder before we start on Fall treats?" Asher asks, gently sliding her down his back and letting her feet land on the soft earth.

Hazel frowns as she collects the apples on the ground and drops them into the basket. "Oh, okay."

I give Asher a nudge before crouching down next to Hazel. "Don't listen to that old grump. You and I can make whatever you want," I whisper.

Hazel beams and bounces on the spot. "Really? Can we make some tonight?"

Asher chimes in with an unusual undertone. "Oh, um... We can't tonight. But maybe this weekend."

I raise a suspicious brow, but he shrugs, and I don't question it. It has been a busy day already. Maybe he wants to relax when we get back to the ranch.

"Oh, yeah!" Hazel's sudden outburst feels more like an afterthought to something they aren't telling me.

I pitch Asher a perplexed smile. "Is there something going on tonight that I don't know about?"

"Oh, you know... I was going to see where the night takes us," Asher replies, pulling me for a quick kiss on the temple. He takes Hazel's hand and motions for me to follow them deeper into the orchard. "Let's try over here. We shouldn't pick so many from the same tree."

I nod in agreement and follow along, tilting my head back to take in the warm breeze blowing through the full, leafy trees. Hazel has been looking forward to apple-picking all week, and Asher and I decided that if there's ever an opportunity to make new memories together, today would be the perfect day for it.

Memories like these give life meaning and mold us into the people we become later in life. I hope Hazel can look back on these times when she's older and feel the same love for this old orchard as I do.

"Dad, what about that one!"

I lower my eyes to see Hazel pointing up at a large tree ahead, bursting with pops of pinks and yellows. A smile crosses my lips. She can always spot the best apples. Just like I could when I was her age.

"Good eye," Asher says before lifting her back onto his shoulders. When the two get closer, Asher calls me over. "Babe, you have to come see this!"

Thinking Hazel must have found another one with a worm in it, I suck in a deep breath and slowly inch my way towards them. "What is it? *Please* don't tell me it's another worm."

Asher lowers himself to draw Hazel out of the flurry of green leaves. I look up, half expecting to throw up in my mouth, but instead of holding an apple, Hazel has something else in her hand. Something red and square.

*A ring box?*

"Asher..."

He sets Hazel down on the ground before taking the box from her. His face is broad with a smile as he drops a kiss on the top of her head. "*Excellent job, Sweetpea.*"

I'm speechless.

All I can do is stare with wide eyes and a mouth hung open as he lowers onto one knee in front of me. It's the moment I've been waiting for the last six months, but how did I not see it coming?

Hazel stands beside Asher, fidgeting from excitement as she looks between me and her dad.

"I've been wanting to do this since the night we went star gazing," he says, holding the velvety red box in one hand and my hand in the other. A nervous smile crosses his face. "Gemma, you're the love of my life. It didn't take me long to figure out that you were someone very special to me. No one has ever made me feel this complete. You took the parts of me that were broken and put them back together again. You're my best friend."

Something in his voice catches, and he pauses for a moment, wiping an eye with the back of his hand.

"Then, I saw how you fixed those same parts in Hazel. That's when I knew I wanted you in our lives forever... But I guess you already knew all that. I'm just sorry I made you wait so long before asking."

Oh my gosh. This is it. He's about to ask!

I look down at Hazel, and her eyes are misty with tears.

*Oh, good grief, please don't let her cry!*

If she cries, I'll *definitely* cry. Then, Asher will cry. And soon, we'll all be one big crying mess! All three of us share a nervous laugh and my heart rate spikes when Asher finally opens the box to reveal a beautiful gold-banded engagement ring.

And not just any ring, either. *My ring.* It's the same one I've been drooling over since I entered the wedding dress business.

My hand flies to my mouth in shock as the white oval diamond glistens in the sun. But how did he—?

"Marry me, Gemma. And make me the happiest man alive. What do you say?" Asher looks up at me with pure hope in his eyes.

"Yes! *Absolutely*, yes!"

"Yeah! All right!" Hazel cheers and claps as Asher lets out a sigh of relief and slides the dazzling ring onto my shaky finger.

When he pushes to his feet, he pulls me in and gazes deep, deep into my eyes, making my knees feel like they might buckle under me at any moment. "I love you, baby," he whispers.

"I love you," I reply, wrapping my arms around his neck and crashing my lips against his.

Hazel makes a retching sound and covers her eyes as Asher leans into the kiss, placing one hand on my back and the other on the back of my head as he holds me close with a promise never to let me go.

Finally, we stop for air and he lifts me, giving me a sudden playful spin before returning me back down to the ground. "I'm going to spend the rest of my life making every memory with you count. Glad you decided to stick around and take a chance on this lonely country boy from Tennessee."

"Who'd thought you'd fall for some uppity city girl. *And* the boss's daughter, no less."

"Not me," he says cooly. "But I sure don't regret it."

I place my hand on his cheek and search his eyes. "No. Can't say I do either."

"Good." Asher wraps an arm around me and pulls Hazel in for the world's longest three-way hug.

"You're married!" she exclaims with arms wrapped around our waists.

Asher laughs. "That's not really how all this works, Sweetpea. We still have a wedding to plan."

With all the excitement, I haven't even thought about the work to plan a wedding. With Fall just around the corner, I'll be swamped with new orders. And Asher is about to start the peak of rodeo season. We need to pick out a venue and hire a caterer. I have to tell Olivia. Oh, and I need to start designing a dress!

As if he were a professional poker player reading my hand of cards, Asher snaps me out of my freight train of endless thoughts. "Whatever you want, it's yours. We can fly in the best wedding planner in Texas if we need to, and your dad's already given me his word that it'll be the biggest wedding this town has ever seen. You tell me what you need, and I'll make sure you have it," he assures me.

"Can I throw flowers?" Hazel asks, tugging at the bottom of my shirt with puppy dog eyes.

"Duh! I can't have a wedding without a flower girl. You can even help me design your dress."

"Woo hoo!" Hazel breaks away to celebrate with a victory dance, and my eyes fall to the ring on my hand.

"Did I do good?"

"Of course. But... how did you know?"

"Oh, let's just say a few little birds told me."

"Sam and Olivia? I *knew* it! I love how they drag me into every ring store in a fifty-mile radius to show me what *they* like, only to go behind enemy lines and sell my secrets."

"Hey, I'm not the enemy. At least, not anymore... Right?"

"Well, you do have impeccable taste in women. I suppose that's got to count for something."

Asher leans his forehead against mine just as a gentle breeze rustles the leaves overhead, and I can't think of a better place for a memory like this than the apple orchard I've loved since I was a kid. He really did make this the best proposal ever.

"I can't wait to be your wife, Mr. Davidson."

Asher smiles and brushes a thumb over my slightly flushed cheek. "We'll get on that as soon as possible, future Mrs. Davidson."

The best thing about the future is that it's full of possibilities. With nothing to regret and nothing left to forget, it's a bottomless wishing well of hopes and dreams, and I have so much to look forward to with this grumpy cowboy by my side.

**THE END**

# More Clean Romance from Ava

*Did you like this book?*

Sign up for my newsletter and read
**My Best Friend's Grumpy Brother** for free.

**H**e was enemy #1 – a grumpy critic set to destroy my career—Until the night we got stuck together, *and he kissed me.*

And just wait until my best friend finds out the hunky dad I've been shacked up with is her little brother.

I better start running now!

The plan was to quit my job and open my own restaurant.

But plans changed when some faceless food blogger started coming after me.

I knew I had to find this miserable little internet troll before he destroyed my rep.. And my sanity.

Ok. I'll admit it.

Showing up on his doorstep to confront him on the verge of the biggest snowstorm of the year was NOT part of my master plan.

But love can be confusing.

And it was only a matter of time before this drop-dead gorgeous mountain man and the precious little girl that called him daddy made me question everything I thought I knew about him.

And myself.

## Find my full library of books on Amazon:

· ♥ · ♥ · ♥ · ♥ · ♥ ·

**Faking With My Brother's Best Friend**

**The Grumpy Cowboy Next Door**
**(Book Two in The Sugar Plum Series)**

Stay tuned for future updates on the next stand-alone novel in The Sugar Plum Series (Coming Summer of 2024)

**Follow me on Facebook and Instagram**
**@AvaWakefieldRomance**

Printed in Great Britain
by Amazon